wayward

"This riveting, many-layered story shines on all levels.
Gabe's first-person narration brilliantly (and with humor)
captures the tone of an angry, confused tween without being over
the top, and his metamorphosis from powerless to empowered
is both realistic and compelling. The coyote's story adds depth and
poignancy. As a story about community, healing, and
family—both human and animal—this is one of the best."
—*KIRKUS REVIEWS* (starred review)

"Lorentz illustrates how change can come from pain
and that there is a path forward, even from the worst situations.
The characters and friendships are realistic, as are the emotions Gabe
feels. An accessible example of positive approaches to restoration
and an excellent tale of relationships and community."
—ALA *BOOKLIST*

"Overall, this book has excellent messaging about navigating
friendship challenges, dealing with hard consequences, and the
importance of surrounding yourself with supportive people."
—*SCHOOL LIBRARY JOURNAL*

"Carl Hiaasen meets Rebecca Stead in this insightful,
touching, funny, and as simple as possible but no simpler novel . . .
by which I mean, it has the exact right number of elements, no
wasted brush strokes, nothing extraneous. It all adds up to a page-
turning story that is both new and familiar—timely and timeless—
at the same time. I loved it from beginning to end."
—CHRIS TEBBETTS, #1 *New York Times* bestselling
coauthor of the Middle School series

WAYWARD
CREATURES

DAYNA LORENTZ

CLARION BOOKS
AN IMPRINT OF HARPERCOLLINS PUBLISHERS
BOSTON   NEW YORK

Clarion Books is an imprint of HarperCollins Publishers.

Wayward Creatures

The Library of Congress Cataloging-in-Publication Data is on file.
ISBN 978-0-06-329091-4

Typography by Kaitlin Yang
Cover design by Kaitlin Yang

23 24 25 26 27   PC/CWR   10 9 8 7 6 5 4 3 2 1

First paperback edition, 2023

FOR MY BROTHER, JORDAN

ONE
Rill

MY NOSE TO THE GROUND, I track the marmot through the leaves. It's a big one—a perfect meal for my pack. Even better, these things are slow, meaning there's some chance that my good-for-nothing, lazy-as-mud-on-the-riverbank siblings might actually catch it.

"Birch! Pebble!" I yip. I've driven the marmot into a hollow. If my brothers and sister come down from every side like we'd barked about, it's over. We feast!

"I've got it!" howls Pebble, who comes bumbling out of the exact wrong bush *behind* the marmot.

"No!" I snap. "You need to get in front of it! Sand! Fern!"

Birch leaps out from a different bush—into the wrong hollow. "Where is it?" he yips, waving his bushy tail.

Burrs and prickers . . . I race past Pebble, driving the marmot on, hoping these fuzz-brains will catch up, but when I break through the brush, I see how far off the scent I am with that dream: instead of two waiting sets of jaws ready to pounce, Sand and Fern are down in the dried-out creek bed, rolling in the soft earth.

"Get off, Sand! It's my stick."

"Come and get it, Fern-frond!"

I am so flabbergasted by their total failure as hunters that I break from my chase and just gape at the roiling gold-and-red fur ball that is their two bodies.

The marmot glances back at me, squeals, and tears across the duff-covered ground, disappearing into the dense brush on the other bank.

I'm growling before I even think to growl, that's how angry I am. I could literally kill and eat my siblings at this point. I mean, if this was the first hunt they'd messed up, it'd be one thing, but this is more like the thousandth hunt they've ruined for me.

"We just lost breakfast because of you!" I snap, running straight into Fern and knocking him into Sand.

"Come on, Rill," Sand says, rolling to his feet. "Stop being such an alpha-licker." *Alpha-licker* is Sand's name for any coyote who actually listens to Mother and Father. "Bet you can't get the stick." He tosses it in his jowls, taunting me. Fern, who's a runt, leaps at the stick, and Sand flicks his head to keep Fern from snatching it.

"You do not want to mess with me, Sand. You just ruined a perfect setup with a delicious marmot."

He flicks his tail, leaps to the other side of the bank. "So you admit I'm the alpha of this stick?"

"I'm the stick alpha!" Pebble howls, diving out of a bush and flattening Sand. She rips the stick from his teeth and trots down the dry bed, her tall ears pointed front and her nose high.

Honestly, these pups will never learn. I leap over Fern and land my front paws on Pebble's hindquarters, sending her sprawling forward. I yank the stick out of her jowls, then sit on the edge of the bank. "The ears have to always be turning, on the lookout for danger."

Birch pounces on my tail. "Your ears didn't hear me coming!"

I whip around to get him, but then the whole mess of them are on me, yipping and licking and nibbling my fur. I take after Father—tall with a thick coat of silvery-brown fur—while these pups are all golden-red like Mother, but once the pups push me into the dry bed, the dust flies and soon the whole pack of us is covered and dull brown.

"What is this?" The sharp bark cuts through our play. *Mother.* "You all are making quite a signal for any humans in the woods." I'm about to remind her that we haven't even seen a human here since we arrived last moon, but then Mother yips, her voice sliding into disbelief. "Rill? Are *you* involved in this?"

The pups stop attacking me. The dust settles. I stand a shoulder above my siblings, the lone survivor of Mother's first litter.

"We were just playing for a second," I begin, but her eyes cut me off.

"I expect more from you, Rill. Yearling coyotes help train the new litter—they don't become a part of it." Mother turns her snout to glare at the dust-covered pups. "You all," she snaps, "back to the den and groom yourselves."

I turn to follow them.

"Not you," Mother growls. "You find some food for your siblings. Remember your place in this pack." She lopes after the pups.

I'm so stupid—how could I let them drag me into their play? I know my job: I'm their teacher; I'm the one who has to make sure that they survive. After what happened to Boulder and Maple—I know better, *I know better . . .*

I try to pick up the scent of the marmot. I'll catch it myself.

Our pack used to live in a bigger forest, along the edges of the human dens. I was born in deep, dark woods, near a waterfall. It was just me and my two brothers: Mother and Father's first litter. My parents had managed to claim that patch of territory only after wandering far from their parents' territories in even wilder woods. They'd never seen a human up close, though they'd heard tales of them. So they didn't know about their traps, didn't know enough to tell us to avoid them.

Boulder and Maple got trapped one evening while we were hunting as a family—well, Mother and Father were hunting, and we three were just messing around. As we tumbled into a clearing, Boulder smelled meat hidden under the leaves. How was he to know? The trap snapped. Another caught Maple. I howled for help. The human jumped out; it'd been watching. I bolted for the cover of the trees, terror pumping through me. Mother and Father attacked, tried to save Boulder and Maple, but the human had a fire stick that blasted noise and made the ground pop and the air bite. Mother, Father, and I scrambled away, thinking we could come back and help Boulder and Maple when the fire stick stopped flashing. But when quiet fell and we returned, they were gone.

So Mother is right: I do know better than to let my guard down. What am I teaching these pups? How are they ever going to survive?

The marmot has disappeared. I hunt up a few mice, collect them in my jowls, and lope back to the den.

TWO
Gabe

THE ALARM GOES OFF AND I must have hit snooze one too many times because I look at the clock and it's 7:15 a.m. I jump out of bed—the school bus pulls up to my stop at 7:50 sharp —rip open my door, and see that the bathroom door across the hall is shut. Inside, I hear Liz humming to herself in the shower. So I dash up the hall into my parents' room, but Dad is in their bathroom shaving.

"I need to use the bathroom," I tell him.

"You see I'm using it," he says, his reflection glancing at me.

"But Liz is in ours and I have to get to the bus."

"Get up earlier," he says.

Thanks, Dad. Helpful. His shift doesn't even start until ten —he was laid off last spring and now is just working part-time at a hardware store.

I stomp out of their room thinking how it used to be that Mom made sure I was up at 6:45. Now, she's too busy getting herself ready—she's had to become the full-time breadwinner. Now, no one in this family has time for anyone but themselves.

In the hall I pass Liz, who's draped in towels. "Hog the bathroom much?" I snap.

She ignores me as usual, slams the door to her room. She's a senior in high school and thinks that makes her important.

I slam the bathroom door shut just to let her know it doesn't.

"Stop slamming doors!" Mom screams from downstairs.

The bathroom is thick with steam, and my pjs stick to my skin. I don't have time to shower, so I peel off the clothes and slap water on my face and under my arms in the name of Not Smelling. Some guys can get away with stink—tall guys, sporty guys, guys who have something else they can be known for, like that guy who learned to unicycle. Me, I'm average everything with dull, straight brown hair, baby-fat cheeks, and gray-blue eyes a girl once described as "colorless." If I smell, it'll be the most interesting thing about me, and suddenly I'm "Pigpen" or "Sir Stinks-a-Lot" or "BO Boy."

I open the window to let out some of the fog and see the light on in Owen's room. His house is up a street on the corner. We've known each other forever. We did a project last spring on Morse code, and he had this idea to test it one night using flashlights—me in this window and him in his room. It was so cool, we decided to blink messages to each other every night after our parents went to sleep. But then school ended, and he and Leo, my other best friend, went to sleep-away soccer camp for the whole summer, and now we're in junior high and haven't seen much of each other. Owen and Leo are playing in this private soccer league—Nordic Post—so they're always at training or practice or traveling to games. I told Mom and Dad that I had to join Nordic Post at least for training, begged even, but they were like, *Do you know how expensive that is?* Which is "No" in parent-speak. Meanwhile Liz asks them for SAT lessons and they're like, *Sure!*

I've tried blinking my flashlight at Owen at our old meet-up time a few nights. He never answers.

Back in my room, I hunt through my drawers for something decent to wear. It's come down to that: the right shirt makes or breaks my day. And of course everything I like is dirty. Mom decided that since she had to go back to work full-time, laundry had to become a "family responsibility." It was Liz's week to do laundry. I mentioned to Mom that Liz didn't do any laundry this week, and Mom said, "Liz has extra classes for the SAT." Like that's a legitimate excuse.

Bottom diving in the hamper it is. I strike gold. My favorite shirt and . . . it smells fine! Nothing a little deodorant can't fix. I put it on, and only then notice the ketchup stain.

Perfect.

I rip the shirt off and slam it into the hamper. The plastic bin ricochets off the back wall of the closet and tumbles out onto the floor, barfing clothes.

Perfectperfectperfect.

"GABE!" Mom shouts from downstairs. "MOVE IT!"

"I'M COMING!"

I kick the clothes-barf back into the hamper and then shove it into the closet. When the hamper threatens to tumble out again, I kick it, and it bounces back like a punk, so I kick it harder—and my foot breaks a hole in the plastic.

PERFECT.

Jaw clenched, I turn the stupid hamper around so the hole is in the back and carefully close the closet door. I fish the only remaining clean outfit from my dresser: a weird green T-shirt and my least favorite track pants with mismatched socks.

The kitchen is in the usual state of morning chaos. Mom and Dad are talking at each other about who's the busier parent and why the other should be responsible for picking up Liz after her away game. Their schedules are so crazy, they didn't fight me on quitting Hebrew school this year, which had always been non-negotiable before. But now, I guess everything having to do with me is negotiable. I almost miss Hebrew school.

"What should I eat?" I ask.

"Find something," Dad snaps.

I prefer the old Dad, before he lost his job, back when he just ignored the rest of us. Now, that's Liz's role—she's at the table with headphones on, glued to her phone while drinking coffee and eating her fancy muesli. I find my cereal in the pantry, and there are only like five flakes rattling around.

"My cereal's dead," I say to no one in particular.

"Put it on the list," Mom says from across the room, and continues to be barked at by Dad about how he has an interview today and shouldn't that be the priority? It's like he's mad at her for getting a job, like it's her fault he got fired.

"But what can I eat?" I say, still staring into the pantry.

"Gabe, there are two other boxes of cereal in there." Mom takes the empty box from my hands and tosses it in the recycling. "Pick one of those."

I run my fingers over the cardboard tops. We've switched to generic cereals, all except for Liz's muesli. Her box even feels different.

I take out the muesli box, shaking it as I walk to the counter just to up the drama. No one looks. I find a bowl. Nothing from the audience. I dump the rest of that disgusting plant grit into the bowl. Every. Last. Grit.

Finally, the audience speaks. "Mom!" Liz whines. "He's eating all my muesli!"

Warmth like lava spreads inside. I dump milk on the mush, and it looks so freaking gross. I make a show of dipping a spoon in, touching my tongue to it.

"This is disgusting," I say, and promptly dump the whole bowl of sludge into the trash.

"Mom!" Liz exclaims.

"Enough!" Dad interjects. "Could you two just stop?"

The fumes of rage are visibly radiating off Liz. My work is done.

I grab a granola bar from the pantry and sit opposite Liz.

"It was your week to do laundry." I throw the words across the table.

Liz doesn't even look up. "You have clothes."

"But it was your week and you didn't do it."

"Can't you see I'm in the middle of something?" She flicks her eyes up at me, then looks back at her phone.

All that glow of gloat I'd had, every bit of it, seems to have blown away on my journey from counter to table. The granola bar tastes like dirt. Mom and Dad have moved from shouting to slamming cabinet doors. I head out to wait for the bus.

A couple fifth-graders are standing at the stop with a little kid, maybe in third grade. The older kids are saying something to the little guy, and he's getting red in the face, clenching his hands into fists. I am so sick of people fighting, so I scream, "Leave him alone!"

The three of them look at me. One guy snorts and sizes me up, then he and his buddy huddle together. The little guy gives me this half-smile, like a thank-you, but also like he's scared of me.

It's the middle of September, and the air is sharp even though the leaves are just beginning to turn. A couple of birds dart around in the branches above the stop. Back when I was little, I remember Mom sitting with me at the kitchen window, watching the bird feeder. We made up silly names for all the birds that came through: the Greater Eastern Yellow-bellied Pointy-beak, Queen Aurelia's Peeping Cheepy-cheep. I know their real names now: goldfinch, chickadee. Our names were better.

Kids begin crowding the stop. Even with all that noise, my stupid ears home in on Owen's and Leo's voices behind me.

"When Parker head-butted that goal? Sick."

"If he can do that at the game, forget it."

"Hey," Owen says to me as he slides up to the stop.

I'm so surprised that he acknowledged my existence, the word "Hey" just pops from my mouth. Usually, I'm running to the bus just as it pulls up. Owen and Leo are always already on it and in a seat together when I climb on. It's weird, but I don't even try to sit near them. It's easier to just sit on my own, stare out the window.

"How's it hanging in Allen?" Leo says, kicking the telephone pole.

Ethan Allen is the name of my house at East Burlington

Junior High. They're both in Samuel de Champlain, the other house. It means that they rotate among one group of teachers, and I rotate among another set. The official idea is that the students have a "more intimate seventh-grade experience": smaller classes with fewer different kids in each and teams of teachers dedicated to those fewer kids specifically. Whoever had this great idea forgot that for some kids, it would mean being trapped with a bunch of strangers while all your best friends get to hang out without you.

"Awesome Allen," I say, voice dripping with sarcasm, and give a feeble little pump with my arms. It's the house catchphrase. We have to say it at every all-school meeting as a sign of our "House Pride."

Leo snorts a laugh. "I hear Ms. Brussels assigns mountains of homework."

"I had to buy hiking boots," I say.

They both laugh. Owen gives me this look like he just remembered I exist.

"We were all going to hang after school," he says. "You free?"

This jolt sizzles over me. "You don't have a game?" They're always traveling for games.

"Bye week," Leo says, dribbling a rock between his feet.

"You in?" Owen asks.

"Yeah," I say, a little too quickly, then add, "Sure. Awesome."

"Allen," Leo sing-songs.

THREE
Rill

ANOTHER SUNRISE, ANOTHER FAILED ATTEMPT at a hunt with the runts. "Pebble, Sand, stop fighting over that rock. Fern, get out of the puddle. Birch, stop chasing that beetle and get your nose on this scent." It's like trying to keep a swarm of flies together.

"Aw, Rill, you're better at hunting than we are," whines Sand. "Can't you catch breakfast?"

"Yeah, my tummy's rumbling," whimpers Fern.

"The whole point is for *you* to get better at hunting," I snap.

"You're mean," barks Birch.

"She's always got her fur rumpled about something," Pebble grumbles.

My eye begins to twitch. This has been happening a lot over the past few suns. I can't attack these pups, can't grab them by the scruff and shove their noses into a rodent hole, can't make them do anything. But if I'm not biting at their heels, they just wander off to play. And I'd let them, except Mother and Father bark at me about my role in the pack, about proper coyote behavior—when are they going to start grinding those same messages into the bones of these fuzz-brains?

"Can you please pay attention for one stinking heartbeat?!" I snap.

"The wind is cold," whines Pebble.

"Too cold to hunt," agrees Fern.

"Let's go to the stream," suggests Sand.

"Yay!" yips Birch, and they all start trotting down the hill toward the water.

I'll just hunt my own breakfast. The pups aren't going to get into trouble at the stream—there's hardly any water in it; there hasn't been rain for suns. And I'll save a bite for each of them off whatever I catch.

The scent of rabbit drifts by, and I manage to down the thing in a thicket without much of a chase. I decide to eat right there where I caught it—I hunted the meal; I should get to eat as much as I want.

The rabbit is delicious. My belly's full for the first time in days. The sun shines down through the opening in the treetops, warming my fur. I lounge in the glade, enjoying the peace, the space. No pup running into me. No Mother howling about my responsibility to the pack. Just me and this butterfly. I snap at it and it flutters off.

Standing, I take a long, slow stretch because I feel like it and why not? I'm thirsty, so I guess I should drag the remains of the rabbit to the stream for the runts.

I lope through the leaves, leap over a low bush, and—yikes! —company: I startle a young deer. The hoof-head rears, squealing like a mouse, then bounds away from me. From *me!*

This is the power of the coyote: every other forest dweller knows to keep their distance. I am the top of this food chain —at least here in this patch of forest. Father once told of an unfortunate run-in he had with a bear when he was a pup, but that was far from our new territory. And if I am the top predator in this stack of sticks, why do I need a pack at all? Especially a pack of bumbling, stumbling pups . . .

I shake the thought from my brain. That's not how coyotes should think. Coyotes have obligations to their families, owe their parents respect and their siblings allegiance. What kind of coyote even thinks of running off? *Bad* coyotes.

I pick up my pace. The runts have been alone at the stream for too long. They're going to be hungry, and this rabbit isn't near enough to fill their tummies. I'll have to nip them into a hunt.

"Nice of you to join the pack." Mother stands on the rocky bank, above the stream where the pups cower, eyes wide and tails low, covered in mud.

Oh no. I drop the rabbit. "I just went off to catch—"

"You left them alone!" she snaps. "Any predator could have snatched them up."

"There are no predators in these woods—"

"Don't tell me what is or isn't in the woods," Mother barks. "Just because we haven't found a trap doesn't mean they're not around."

I don't know if it's the wind or the pathetic faces of my muddy siblings or the fact that Mother has not even mentioned the fact that I brought back a rabbit for them, but that twitch in my eye becomes a rockslide in my brain and I snap.

"Enough, Mother!" I yip. "I can't do this anymore."

She tilts her head, considers me with her amber eyes. "Can't do what? Take care of your siblings? That's what we do in a pack—we take care of each other."

"No, that's not what *we* do, that's what *I* do. I'm taking care of these runts, I'm catching all the meals. But no matter how much I do, it's never enough. Nothing I do can ever bring back Maple and Boulder, Mother." I hadn't ever put that thought into barks, but it's been there, always, lurking under everything.

She cringes slightly, hearing those names. "Our pack failed once, and you saw what happened. Don't fail the pack now by choice."

"If everything I do is wrong, aren't I failing now anyway?" I growl.

Father lopes out of the shadows, appears beside Mother. "What's all this howling about?"

"Rill thinks she's better than this pack." Mother glares at me.

"Oh, come now," Father whuffles, panting slightly, as if anything about this is funny. "Rill, I know these pups can be trouble, but we all have to do our part. It's the coyote way. We each have our place in the pack."

"Maybe I don't want a pack," I yip.

Father's ears whip forward, and his tail lifts. "What's that?"

I barked, "*Maybe I don't want a pack!*" I stand tall, chest out.

"Nonsense!" Mother yips.

The pups all gaze up at me with wide amber eyes. Father's head tilts like he's not quite able to hear my barks.

"It's not nonsense," I snap, feeling more certain with every bark. "Father was a lone coyote for a season. I can do it, too."

"Not at your age he wasn't," Mother begins, "and that was out of necessity for his pack. They had too many mouths to feed. *Your* pack needs you here."

"But maybe—" I start before Father barks, "But nothing! Rill, I won't allow it." He sits down and raises his snout like that will put an end to the discussion.

For a moment, I hesitate, feel my paws drawn toward the stream, the need in the pups' eyes to help them clean up, the command in my parents' stances. But then I remember that brief moment in the sun, the power of startling that deer, the delicious languor from a full belly, and it's like the choice was made before we even started barking.

"Goodbye, family," I yip.

I whip around and run, fast and hard, through the trees, over rocks, through thickets of weeds. All I hear is my breath pulsing over my lolling tongue, the pounding of my heart, because I am free; I am the wind and the wild.

Only when I stop at the crest of a hill do I hear the echo of a howl. "Rill!" my mother's voice cries.

But then the wind changes and it's gone.

I'm left alone with the breeze, the birds chirping, a bug zipping by, squirrels chittering. Forest sounds, but not coyote noise.

I snort, shake my fur, clear my body of Mother and Father, of my siblings, of all of it. I leap off the rock into the shadows a new coyote. A pack unto herself.

four
Gabe

AT LUNCH, I LOOK FOR OWEN and Leo—lunch is the only time the two houses combine. The first day, it was so crazy in the cafeteria with everyone rushing to grab tables that I just ran out, clutching my bagged lunch from home. For the past two weeks, I've been eating in the library. But not today. Today, I am finding Owen and Leo, and we will sit together like we used to back in sixth grade.

But I don't see them in the cafeteria. I push through the doors outside and see them on the soccer field with a bunch of other kids. They are all really good at soccer. I used to play, but I was never good. Last fall when Owen, Leo, and I did the town's program, I scored a goal on my own team by accident. These guys? They wouldn't want me even if I asked to play.

I go back inside, through the loud chaos of the cafeteria, and sneak down the hall to the library. I eat slowly, just me and the books and some other kids on the other side of the room who come here for some club.

After school will be different. After school, we're hanging out, just me, Owen, and Leo. Like we used to.

~

The final bell rings and I fly down the stairs, racing toward Owen's locker. I want to catch him and Leo before the bus, to be sure we sit together. But as I turn the corner, I see this other kid standing with them. A tall guy with good hair and clothes that are definitely not hand-me-downs. The kind of kid no one would ever think to call Sir Stinks-a-Lot.

"This is Taylor," Owen says as I approach. I learn Taylor's in Champlain House, that he went to one of the other elementary schools and lives on the other side of town, but he plays Nordic Post with the guys.

A part of me is like, *Uh, weren't "we" as in Leo, Owen, and me hanging out?* But then Owen says, "Taylor's coming over to hang out with us."

Us. As in me, Owen, and Leo. Taylor is hanging out with *us.*

We head out to the bus and find seats together, then start planning the rest of the day.

"Let's ride our bikes over to the park," I say as we bump down Shelburne Road.

Owen gives me this look. "Taylor doesn't have his bike."

And I feel like an idiot. Until Leo says, "I have my old one."

Taylor shrugs. "Cool."

We get off at our stop, and I run home to get my bike. The house is silent, but instead of it being the first moment of the black hole of the weekend, it's like the house is holding its breath to let out this shout because this afternoon is going to be awesome.

Allen.

Ha!

I grab a snack, then three more for the guys, and shove them into a gear bag with my water bottle, then run out through the garage. I bike over to Leo's house, and the guys are all there. Taylor is riding around on this kind of dingy bike, popping wheelies. Owen and Leo are all like, "Whoa!"

Taylor can pop wheelies?

"Hey," I say, and then add, "I brought chips."

The guys turn to me, and Owen holds a hand out. "Awesome."

"Allen," I say in a singsong voice.

No one laughs.

We pass around the bags of chips, and it's kind of fun. They were all different, so we share bags. When Taylor gets the Cheetos, there's nothing left, but he jams his fingers into the creases to pick out the crumbs. He pulls out his hands, which are coated in orange dust.

"Gross," Leo says, but he's smiling.

Taylor curls his fingers into claws and lunges at Leo, saying, *"Bleh bleh!"* like a vampire, and we all laugh.

I crack a Dorito into fangs and jam them under my upper lip. *"I vant to suck your blood,"* I say.

All I get is a smirk from Owen.

Taylor crushes his bag and hands it back to me, empty, like I'm a garbage can. "Let's head out," he says.

Taking a cue from Taylor, Owen and Leo both hand me their bags and peel out after him. It occurs to me that I might have been wrong about the members of the "us" Owen was referring to back at school.

No. He meant me and him and Leo, I'm sure. We've always been *us*.

The guys are already halfway down the block as I scramble onto my bike and start pedaling.

We ride to Veterans Park and climb on the structures. The place is deserted, so we start doing crazy stuff. Leo pulls himself onto the top of one structure and jumps from roof to roof. Owen does a flip off the platform. I run up the slide, catch the bar at the top, and flip over it, landing on my feet.

"But can you do this?" Taylor asks me. Then he backflips off a tube.

"Awesome!" Leo says.

Allen, I think but don't say.

"Dude, can you teach us to wheelie?" Owen says.

Taylor nods. "Sure."

We ride around the parking lot, Taylor showing us how to jerk the handlebars just so. I keep hitting myself in the crotch with my seat.

"Dude, maybe you want to sit this one out," Taylor says, sailing by me on his back wheel.

"Don't call me *dude*," I grumble under my breath.

After fifteen loops, I'm out. But the guys are still at it. I dump my bike by the curb and sit to watch them circle. They're laughing and Owen almost gets it, and then Leo does, so Owen is like, "I am *getting* this," and starts jerking his handlebars like he's going to die if he doesn't pop a wheelie now that Leo has.

I think about jumping back on my bike, getting back into it, but it would look stupid now, so I don't. I finish the last of the water in my bottle. On the opposite side of the street from the park, there's this gas station and mini-mart. "I'm getting a drink," I yell to the guys, but they aren't listening to me.

The mini-mart is empty. There's a guy behind the counter watching TV on his phone. I walk to the back where there's a wall of refrigerators. I stare into the bright glare, train my eyes over the glowing canisters, and then notice in the reflection a shelf behind me with the sign HALF-OFF FIREWORKS. I turn. There are a couple of Roman candles sticking up out of a tube.

I have a vision: Me, shooting fireworks over the guys' heads as they circle on their bikes. Me, better than any wheelie-popper because I have explosives, which by definition are cooler than anything you can do on a bike, obviously. Me, definitely a member of *us*, certainly someone who gets noticed for something other than his stink. I'd be Fireworks Guy, bringer of awesomeness, and Taylor would be the *dude* sitting this one out.

But then I see the catch: there's a small tag under the half-off sign that says: 18 AND UP.

I peer over the top of the shelf. The guy is still glued to his phone. I snatch a handful of Roman candles and shove them up inside my jacket and down into the waistband of my jeans. Then I turn back to the fridge and grab whatever's in front of me. I walk up to the counter and slide the bottle toward the guy. My hands start sweating. *Keep cool . . .*

The guy doesn't look up from the phone, just waves the bottle in front of the scanner, then says, "Two bucks thirty."

I dig three dollars from my backpack and hand them to him, praying he doesn't notice the slight sheen of sweat on the bills. He hits the register, then slides a couple coins back to me. As I pick up the coins, I swipe a book of matches from the carton on the counter. He notices nothing. I slip out the door, then run over the pavement to my bike. Only when I'm back across the street do I breathe, gulping in the air.

"Dude, what are you doing?" Owen has pulled up beside the curb.

"Check this out," I say, lifting my coat so he can see the fireworks.

"Whoa," he begins, lips curling. "Leo! Taylor!"

My mind scrambles for the perfect place to launch my prizes. We need darkness, privacy . . . "We can go to Rockledge Park," I say. It's a "natural area," just a bunch of trees bordering the lake.

"Dude!" Owen says, waving for Leo.

Leo pulls up beside us, and I slide a candle out of my waistband so he can see the label. "Sick!" Leo says.

Taylor pops a wheelie, but neither Owen nor Leo notice. They're looking at me. At what I have.

"Let's go," I say, transferring the fireworks to my backpack, and they both nod. I get on my bike, and Owen yells for Taylor, who's on the other side of the lot, to catch up.

It's very clear who's the *us* and who's the other.

~

We walk our bikes into Rockledge Park. It's the opposite of Veterans Park—there's no playground or grass, just woods and trails and a rocky beach along the lake that becomes cliffs the farther out you go. I lead us into the trees on the main path, far enough that I can't see the lights from the houses that line the edges of the park, and then I stop, slip off my backpack, and pull out one of the Roman candles. The guys—except Taylor, who's still doing wheelies on the dirt—circle around behind me. I light the fuse.

POP POP POP go the fireballs from the canister. They fly up into the shadowy treetops, sparkling between the branches.

The guys go nuts with the first one. Owen whoops, Leo claps, and even Taylor stops riding to check it out. On the second, their voices seem less psyched, like they thought the explosions would be bigger, fly higher. By the third, I see Leo glance over at Taylor.

"Hey, guys," Taylor says, "check this out!" He's wheeling around on his back tire with no hands on the handlebars.

I am so sick of this Taylor kid. Who is he to get up in my and Owen and Leo's hangout? Just some guy they probably wouldn't even be friends with if I hadn't been put in stupid Allen House.

I don't even really think about it. I just light a Roman candle and point it at Taylor and suddenly fireballs are flying at him.

"Yeet!" shouts Leo as one goes by him. Taylor shrieks and dives, bike and all, into a pile of leaves to get out of the way as two more fireballs blaze across the dark.

This laugh escapes my lips, and I feel kind of crazy because I am shooting fireballs at a person.

Taylor climbs out of a bush. "You could have warned me!"

"That. Was. Awesome!" Leo holds a hand out for a Roman candle. "What if we each took one?" he says. "We could, like, duel."

All eyes are back on me. "You up for some revenge?" says Taylor, reaching a hand out.

"Is that safe?" Owen asks, but he's still going for a firework.

"It's fine," I say, because if Taylor wants revenge, then revenge he shall get.

I pass one to each of them, then open the wrapper on mine. I shove an extra firework into my waistband just in case. We all count down together—*three, two, one*—then light them.

POP!

I run from a green flare shooting out of Taylor's tube. Pink, orange, and yellow leave trails across my vision.

POP! POP! POP! POP!

I am on Taylor like a missile: *POP! POP! POP!* And it's weird, but I kind of want to burn him a little, show him that maybe playing with us isn't for guys like him. That maybe he's the odd one out, not me.

He's standing in a patch of dry grass. *Why not?* I lower my candle and shoot a fireball directly into the clump at his feet. The dead blades burst into flames.

Taylor jumps, stamps out the grass. Watching him hop, this sick smirk creeps across my face.

"Are you crazy?" he shouts, once the flames are dead.

"It's just a game, *dude*," I say, a fireball shooting up, lighting my skin green. "Or maybe *you* should sit this one out?" I glare at him.

"Not cool," Taylor says, and joins Owen and Leo's chase.

The three of them are all laughing hysterically, kicking up leaves and snapping branches as they dodge flaming bullets of light. I want to laugh, to even fake laugh, but it's suddenly not funny for me. Why isn't this funny? Am I even having fun?

More pops, more streaks of color. And then heat, crackling. I turn and see that some of the grass where I had shot Taylor's feet is sparking flames. Real flames. Wait—didn't Taylor stamp them all out?

"Guys," I say, but they're jumping and running in circles. A burst of pink shoots from the canister in my hand, drops straight into a thatch of dry weeds. It instantly flares up.

"GUYS!"

I take off my coat, swing it at the weeds, swatting the clump until it stops burning. But then I turn back to the grass, and now more is on fire, and the flames are spreading across the ground, catching twigs and snarls of vines and, oh my god, how is it growing this fast?

"GUYS, STOP!" I pull out my phone. It's off. No, it's dead.

"Holy—" Owen begins.

"We have to get out of here," Leo says, coming up behind me, grabbing my shirt.

"Do you guys have your phones? Mine's dead," I say, panic driving my heart to thumping. My voice cracks. "We have to call someone."

The fire creeps toward a stubby little pine tree and—
FWOOSH!—the whole thing explodes into flame. Heat blasts
my face. Why did it do that? Why would it just explode? This
was just a tiny nothing fire . . .

Leo drops my shirt and stumbles back.

Taylor throws the remnants of his candle. "I am not getting
busted for this." He runs from me, and I turn and see that Owen
and Leo have followed him, that they've all gone, flying into the
dark on their bikes, leaving me alone.

The heat from the fire burns my face. I step back. How did
it get over there? It's everywhere.

I have to stop it. I run for the lake.

FIVE
Rill

THE NIGHT IS QUIET. I wind between the tree trunks, sniffing after a mouse I heard in a patch of dry grass.

There are no other coyote scents in this part of the forest. But I am near the human dens, so that makes sense. Mother and Father would never follow me here. I can really be alone.

Not that they've called for me. I've listened for them all day. They haven't howled for me once since I left. I guess I really am my own pack now.

Good.

I poke my snout into a hole, dig a bit, sniff again. The mouse has escaped. Mice are crafty—they jump in one hole and scurry out another. *This is why we hunt in packs,* I grumble before catching myself. Not my pack. The runts can't concentrate on anything for longer than a few heartbeats. Some packs are useful, maybe, but certainly not mine — my *old* pack.

New noises echo through the trees. *Humans.* It's strange for humans to be in this part of the forest after the sun sinks. They're far enough away, but I'm keeping my ears on them, just to be safe. I drop my nose and begin tracing a spiraling path out from the known mouse hole to find his secret escape hole.

The voices still, followed by explosions of noise — louder than a tree snapping, softer than a thunderclap. What's happening? I climb up a rocky ridge to get a better look at the humans. Another boom, its echo louder. Then a burst of light blinds me. What could be so bright? The flash is followed by a wild wave of noise — scraping and snarling; strange thunder. Then another flash, and another — *BOOM BOOM.* The air fills with a bitter smell that tastes sour.

Birds flee, panicked, their wings beating against the poisoned air. Hooves pound the dirt, making the earth tremble as the deer escape the flashes. Squeals follow the creatures of the earth down into their burrows. Where is a coyote to go?

My den. My pack.

My heart thumps; my mouth is as dry as the riverbed. The flashes and booms continue, and I am frozen on that ledge, my senses thumped again and again by the light, the noise, and the choking stench.

But then a light begins to glow that does not flash. It burns. Burns bright. Grows. The humans become distinct shadows in its light. The flashes stop.

Fire. A forest fire.

Mother told of one caused by lightning when she was a pup, how it burned for days, how she lost part of her pack to its flames.

Do the humans command lightning? Is that what those flashes were?

Yip-yip-yip-yip-HOWL! Father's call. *Fern! Pebble! Birch! Sand!*

The runts. They're separated from Father?

"Father!" Fern barks from somewhere near the lake. Then the rest of my siblings begin yipping, "Father! Mother!" Their voices come from everywhere, like they're spread over the whole of the forest.

They are lost without me.

I can't leave the runts to die. "I'm coming!" I howl. "Fern! Pebble!" I bound off the ledge, race toward the nearest voices. A rabbit scurries past, hopping in the opposite direction as fast as its legs can stretch. Bugs scuttle over the dirt.

"Birch! Sand!" I cry.

A wall of light blooms in front of me, flaring up from the forest floor. What had been leaves and branches is now flame and heat. The fire whirls. It roars.

I rear back, but my fur is singed. The smoke whips out in dark tendrils, choking me. The flames reach for me and I stumble back, but somehow the fire is now behind me, too. The ground burns beneath me, biting my paws. A howl of pain breaks from my throat, my fur now smoldering. The flames are everywhere, smoke closing in around me. I can't breathe.

I race through the flames, not caring which direction, just away from the heat and smoke and ash and burning, across the dirt, through heaps of leaves, up over rocks. I crash through bramble. No matter how much my paws hurt or my lungs burn, I run.

SIX
Gabe

I DROP TO MY KNEES at the edge of the lake and realize I have nothing to put water in. My shoe. That's it! I kick off both my shoes and fill them with water. I stumble up the bank, trying to move fast, but the water keeps sloshing out of my shoes. There's going to be nothing left to douse the fire. But when I get back up to the trail, I see how crazy it was to think I could do anything to stop it.

The whole forest is on fire. Everywhere, red-orange-yellow, swirling and snapping. The flames lick up the trees, crawl across the dry leaves. It touches a birch tree, and the little curls of bark flare all the way up the trunk. The fire makes its own wind, whooshing hot air at me, and the wind burns even though I'm standing far back from the flames.

What did I do?

The fire is so loud and hot and huge that I don't hear the sirens, don't notice a fire truck until it pulls up almost next to me. I drag my bike and backpack out of the road as more trucks come barreling toward me. The firefighters are like superheroes: they get right at it, spraying water from backpack pumps, scraping brush away from the fire's edge. Bells clang from the lake and flashing lights glint through the trees, then new streams of water burst onto the flames from what must be a fire boat. But their tiny hoses and red lights are nothing compared to the fire. Soon, I lose track of them; it's like my brain can only process the flames as they spread and grow.

A hand drops onto my shoulder. "Son, you have to step back." The hand turns me, pulling my eyes and brain from the fire, and I see that the hand belongs to a man in a blue-black uniform, standing beside a white-and-black car with flashing blue lights: a policeman. He stops me and places his other hand on my other shoulder. "Son, what are you doing in here—oh."

I follow his eyes, look down, and there, in my waistband, is the last Roman candle.

"Wait," I say, but he shakes his head, drops his hands.

"Let's wait until your parents are here before you say anything about that." He glances down at the firework. "I'm going to need your name," he says.

"Uh, Gabe." My heart drums against my ribs, in my ears, pulsing with the rhythm of the blue lights.

"Full name, son."

"Gabriel," I say. "Gabriel Meyer."

The fire roars behind me. I see it reflected in the windows of the cop car. It's like the whole world is on fire.

The police officer leans his head over, talks into the walkie-talkie hooked to his shoulder, "Yeah, I have a Gabriel Meyer here. Looks like we found who started the fire."

I want to tell him, *It was an accident,* but my throat is dry and I can't get a word out, only a cough—there's so much smoke. The firelight glints on the cop's belt, and my eyes focus on the silver handcuffs, the yellow Taser, the black outline of his gun.

I remember what Taylor said before he ran: *I am not getting busted for this.* Am I in trouble? Like cops trouble? Kids don't get into cops trouble. What even is cops trouble?

"Son, I need a number for your parent or legal guardian," the officer says.

It's like he's speaking some other language. Why not just say Mom or Dad?

I give him the number for Mom's cell. Then wonder if I should have given Dad's. Who's better with handling cops trouble?

The fire rages. Firefighters are yelling. More trucks show up. More cops. Words bounce around me, and my fingers dig into my jeans like if I just hold on hard enough, it will all stop.

"Gabriel." The cop touches my shoulder.

I whip my face up and look at his hand.

"I need you to get in my car now, son," he says. "Your parents will meet us at the station."

The police station?

I try to walk, but my legs are broken. My socks are wet and my feet are all tingly, and I can't seem to move them from this spot. The cop snatches up my bike and backpack and wet shoes and throws them in the trunk of the cruiser. He then guides me toward the back seat.

"I need to pat you down," he says, stopping my hand as I reach for the door handle.

What? *What?* This is movie stuff, grown-up stuff, not for kids like me, not for me . . .

"Put your hands on the trunk and spread your feet apart."

He pushes me so I fall forward, my hands hitting the metal skin of the car. It's hot against my palms. I shuffle my feet apart. My bladder cinches, and I feel like I might pee my pants. The blue lights flash on my face. I close my eyes as the cop's hands begin patting my shoulders, move on to my armpits, my legs, but I can still see the lights like lightning through my eyelids. He pulls the firework out of my waistband.

"Okay," the cop says. "You can get in." I shuffle my feet together. The fire roars and a tree collapses with a crash. The cop bends my head down. I drop into the seat.

It's not a long drive. I try to shrink down as small as possible, like maybe I can disappear into a crack in the vinyl.

The cop parks the car, opens the back door, and motions for me to get out. He walks me, stumbling, into the station, holding my arm like I might run, like he knows the kind of kid I am: the bad kind. But I didn't run; I tried to help. This was an accident.

The officer leads me back to a desk and sits me in a chair. "Stay here," he says, dropping my wet shoes beside me. They land with a squelch.

The police station is full of people moving around, talking, phones ringing, doors opening and closing. Why is no one running or screaming? Inside me, that's all there is—a screaming whine of panic, frozen, waiting.

"Where is he?" My dad's voice cuts through everything. He sounds angry, his words short and sharp.

He sounds angry at *me*.

I stare at my shoes harder. Doesn't he know it was an accident?

"Over here, sir," the cop says. Then he continues, his voice louder, so I guess they're closer, "I picked him up at Rockledge Park."

"Where the fire is?" Mom asks, voice cracking. "Oh my god, is he okay?"

I'm right here. Why doesn't she speak to me? The scream inside is deafening.

"He's fine, ma'am. We believe he may have started the fire," the cop says. "We found this on him."

She gasps. "We don't own fireworks."

"We would never let him fool around with anything like this," Dad says.

The scream cuts out. Why aren't they defending me?

"The fire marshal believes they have the fire under control. I spoke with the state's attorney and, given Gabriel's age, they don't want to press charges just yet." The *yet* hangs there like a guillotine. "She does want to have your son referred to our community justice center and to have him engage in a restorative justice process. However, your son has to agree to participate."

The process? Restorative justice? But I didn't mean for the whole world to go up in flames.

"What happens if he agrees?" Mom asks.

And I hear it: my mother absolutely believes I did this. On purpose.

My parents are not here to save me. They're just like this cop—there's a fire and there's me and there's a firework in my waistband: done and done. They don't want to hear my side. They think I'm the kind of kid who starts fires on purpose.

The cop answers, "Assuming he successfully completes their process, this case will be dismissed."

"He'll agree to it," Dad says, like I'm not sitting right here.

"That's all up to Gabe."

I feel the weight of their eyes on the back of my head. Like they're daring me to say no.

A part of me wants to throw it in their faces, say, *No way, take me to court, you want to treat me like some criminal, like I did this on purpose, fine, go all the way.* But there's this other part of me, and it feels small, but also, like, it's most of me, and it's brittle, and just hearing the way my parents are talking — half-scared, half-angry, all laced with this tone like they don't know me, or don't want to know me — their words are hitting it like a bat. And that part can't take anymore. Like one more word and it might shatter.

The cop pulls a packet of paper from a file on his desk. "Here's the contact information for the center. If you want to pursue this, call them Monday. Otherwise, we'll send the file to the state's attorney."

My parents take the packet, sign some forms, and then they walk out. At the double glass doors leading outside, Mom turns and looks back.

"Come on, Gabriel," she snaps.

I shove my feet into my wet shoes and stumble out the doors. Neither of my parents look at me. They just get in the car and wait for me to follow. We drive home in silence, like they're daring me to say anything. The streetlights flash over us in slices of orange.

Dad parks in the driveway. "You're grounded," he says.

"Of course he's grounded," Mom says.

They don't even ask what happened. Not even here, parked in the driveway, where there's no cop there to judge their parenting. They don't care that it was an accident. Or that if it wasn't an accident, then it was Taylor's fault, and Leo's and Owen's, not just mine. They don't bother to ask if I'm okay or if I'm completely freaking out. It's like I don't even matter, like I'm just a problem they need to solve.

I get out of the car and walk in the front door and just go straight into my room. I drop onto my bed and bury my face in the pillow because no one—*no one*—will hear me cry about this.

seven
Rill

FEAR AND PANIC PUSH MY legs, nip me onward through the trees. I run until my nose pokes out between the dry stalks of tall weeds and into open space and fresh air. Smooth grass cools my burned paw pads. I pant, heaving in gulps of the clean air. My heart slows; the panic begins to ebb.

It takes several of these slow heartbeats for me to realize that this is one of the made fields around the human dens. My eyes hurt and my vision is blurry, but yes, there is the den, rising like a dark mass, blocking the stars. Squares of light shining from inside the den glow in patches on the grass. And then I see them.

Tall silhouettes, a few stretches away from me: the humans are outside.

My heart races back up, pounding in my ears. I glance

around—there has to be somewhere to hide. For all the clean air, my nose is still clogged with smoke, so I can't smell a way out. My eyes water and can't focus.

One of the silhouettes—smaller, rounder—stumps toward me on short legs. It warbles as it reaches out one of its long limbs.

I have to get away, but where? Back toward the fire? No, I can't. Toward the human den? Never. I have to find someplace safe. But I can't smell the forest, I can't smell what's safe, it's all smoke and fire.

Another warble, so close—the small human is almost on me. Its paws stretch and grab near my eyes. I snap a warning, "Get away!"

The small human screams.

The bigger humans—the tall, terrifying silhouettes—come running toward us.

I have no choice.

I dart back through the dry weeds, back into the forest, back toward the smoke. I'm trapped between the fire and the humans.

"Father!" I howl. "Mother!" I'm desperate, so desperate I'd take even their help.

But there is no answer. Has the fire gotten them? Or have they escaped? Or do they not answer me out of spite . . . It doesn't matter now—if the humans come to hurt me, I am on my own.

I push my legs to keep running, but they fight me every

stretch. The dirt bites my paws, each stick and rock a fang through my skin. The air becomes thick, a cloud of black, and I can no longer breathe. Gasping, coughing, I pad forward, one step, two. Suddenly, my paws hit nothing. My legs lack the strength to stop the fall. I tumble into a gully between the rocks. It's cool and wet, and the smoke seems to float over the small space.

I try to push myself up, but my strength is gone. There's also a sharp pain—a new one, not the bite of the burn, but a throb in my shoulder.

I guess this is where I stay.

I curl my body in on itself, wrapping my tail over my nose as I usually do to sleep, but then flip it away—my fur smells of the fire. I don't need a reminder of what's coming for me. I don't want to smell the fire until I don't have the choice.

My eyes close and my body shivers.

The fire will come for me. And I must simply wait for it. Alone.

eIGHT
Gabe

I DON'T GO DOWNSTAIRS for dinner. Mom knocks and asks if I want a plate. I don't answer.

I can't sleep. Every time I close my eyes, I see the pulse of blue lights, the red burn of the flames. But I must doze a little, because the next time I open my eyes, the sky is dull gray.

The house is quiet. I sneak downstairs and grab a granola bar. Then I take the whole box out of the pantry and creep back up to my room. I take a bite of the bar, and it tastes like cardboard. I wrap the rest of the bar in the foil packaging and put it back in the box.

I check my phone—no texts or emails. Nothing from Owen or Leo.

How could they leave me with a forest fire and not look back once? Who does that? Cowards. Not real friends.

But they haven't been my real friends in months.

I climb back into bed and pull the covers over my head. My brain won't drop the pulsing and the flames, so I try to trick it into thinking about something else — song lyrics. It takes me five different songs until I land on "Baby Shark" and just repeat the lyrics over and over until finally my brain shuts down.

~

"I cannot believe you!" Liz's words shatter the quiet.

I stay under the covers, eyes closed.

"Of all the insane things you could have done to get attention, you decide getting arrested is the best way?!"

Like I need another person to pile on the hate.

"Mom and Dad are completely freaking out! I mean, they had to pick you up at the police station. What were you thinking?!"

Her words hammer into me. I did want attention — but Owen's, Leo's. Is that so bad?

She keeps going, "Ugh, of course you weren't thinking. Some of your loser friends were there, I bet, right? You're so desperate to get back in with them, you decide to set fire to a park like a lunatic?"

Bad, bad. The words pulse in blue light. Is that why the guys ran off? Did they sense it, with me shooting the fireworks at Taylor? It felt insane then. Is that what they saw — see? *Desperate, lunatic, bad . . .*

"You need to check your damage, Gabe, because this is just—"

"GET OUT!" I scream. The words bubble up from my gut, claw up my throat, explode out of my mouth.

"I'm not even in your room, idiot."

In one motion, I leap out of my bed, cross the room, and slam the door. Right in her face.

She screams, "Mom! He broke my nose!" Her footsteps slap down the steps.

This smile creeps out across my lips, a gross smile; and I know it's awful, but for sure I'm smiling because I hurt my sister. Because that's what I wanted, for her to hurt. For her to feel this sickness inside, even just a little.

Who would want that? The kind of kid who thinks about burning another kid. With stolen fireworks. A bad kid.

That's why Owen and Leo ran. They saw this bad kid and ran as far away as possible. The cop saw it. Mom and Dad see it. Liz sees it.

I'm the bad guy. I am the sickness.

That brittle part? It breaks. It's kind of a relief. At least I'm not going to hurt anymore.

Everyone thinks I'm a bad guy? Then I'll be the bad guy.

You hate me? I hate you.

I mean, honestly, who is Liz to get in my face about anything? If she hadn't been so selfish, maybe there would have been a little air in the house for my problems. Maybe if Mom and Dad had taken a second to stop fighting, they would have seen how bad things have been for me. Owen and Leo could have stopped by once just to say hi before school, or texted to meet up for lunch, or just saved me a seat on the bus. If anyone had even bothered to notice anything beyond their own stupid lives, I would never have been in that forest with those fireworks. No way would I have been so . . . desperate. No way any of this would be happening.

~

When the morning light brightens the fabric of my comforter, I get up to use the bathroom.

I crack open my door, check the hall. It's clear. I sneak across, pee, then decide to risk slipping down to the kitchen — I polished off the granola bars last night. I stop at the bottom of the stairs and peek around the corner.

Mom and Dad are sitting at the table with mugs. Not talking. Papers crowd the table's surface.

"I just can't believe this is happening," Mom says. "Where did we go wrong?"

I don't wait to hear what Dad says.

I go back to my room. Close the door. Crawl under the covers.

I don't cry. I won't cry.

I.

Will.

Not.

Cry.

~

Knock at the door. "Gabe?"

It's Mom.

"You need to eat something."

I guess she hasn't noticed the missing granola bar box.

"We should talk."

Nope.

"I'm going to call the community justice center tomorrow," she says. "We're going to get through this."

We, she says, like they are a part of this. Like now that the police are involved, they care. Like now that I'm going to juvie, I'm worth their time.

~

Monday, I get up with the sun, shower, grab food and a water bottle, and am out the door without having to speak to anyone. I am so not doing the bus, so I bike all the way across town to the school. It's cold, and the air freezes my skin, my eyeballs, the snot in my nose. I don't care. I like the hurt.

As I'm locking my bike up outside school, I feel a tap on my shoulder.

"Dude, Gabe," the person says.

I glance back. It's Taylor.

"I need to know what you told the cops."

He's holding on to my shoulder and looking super intensely into my face. It's kind of freaking me out.

"What?" I say. "Nothing."

"Did you tell them I was there?"

His nails dig into my skin through my sweatshirt.

"No," I say, my heart hammering. Sweat pricks out of every pore. "I didn't say anything to them."

He holds on to my shoulder for a second more, then lets go, giving me a little push. "Okay, good," he says, running his fingers through his hair. "Okay," he says again. "I mean, thanks." He backs away from me. "My dad, he would, like, lose it if he knew."

I don't say anything. Like my dad didn't lose it?

"Cool, well, bye," he says, like this was just a regular conversation. Then he runs into the school like he can't get away from me fast enough.

I just stand there, shivering with the amount of effort it's taking for me to not scream or cry or both.

The bell rings.

I suck all that scream back in, all those tears. I shove them down, crush them deep, deep, deep, and then run for the doors.

Inside, I see Taylor huddled with Owen and Leo, whispering.

So they're all in on it.

Walking down the hall, I keep my head in my hoodie, my

hands balled into fists in the pockets. In class, the teacher tells me to take the hood off, so I do, but I keep my head down. Still, I hear the whispers, feel the eyes crawl over me like spiders.

Everyone knows.

I don't go to the cafeteria at lunch. I grab a bagel from the salad bar and eat under the stairs at the bottom of the stairwell with my headphones in. I don't listen to anything, just sit in the semi-darkness and pull bits off the bagel.

In English, I get a text from Mom: *We have an intake appointment at 3. I'll pick you up in front of the school.*

In front of the school? What, so I can be stared at by every single person as they file out?

Absolutely not.

I google the East Burlington Community Justice Center. It's not far.

I have my bike, I text back. *I'll meet you there.*

The little bubble with the dots appears. Disappears. Reappears. Disappears. Then finally Mom chooses words: *Fine. Be there at 3 sharp.*

Like I need something poking me in the back now— something sharp—to keep me in line.

~

It's not until I turn off the bike path onto the street that I discover that the East Burlington Community Justice Center is on the back side of the police station. The website should warn people about this: that to get there, you have to pass by the cops.

The justice center has its own little sign beside its door with a rainbow curling around the words like this place is the nicer, friendlier cousin of the police station on the other side of the wall. This only makes me more suspicious.

Inside, there's a beige room with some beige couches and low wooden tables with pamphlets like *Restoring Communities* and *Repairing Harm versus Punishing Wrong*. Both Mom and Dad are sitting in stiff black plastic chairs with their backs to the window. Mom has her purse in her lap and her hands folded on top of it. Dad has his leg crossed on his knee. He switches legs as I walk in.

"You're late," Dad says.

This meeting is already awesome.

Allen.

I want to smack my brain.

The wall opposite them has a square cutout like they have in doctors' offices. A lady with dirty-blond hair wearing jeans and a fleece pokes her head through.

"We're all here? Fantastic. Come on in," she says.

The door next to the cutout buzzes. I follow my parents through it.

The lady leads us to a small room that's just a circle of chairs and a little table with a folder on it, which the lady sits next to. I take a seat on the opposite side of the room from my parents.

The lady flashes a smile like she's selling knockoff goods and knows it. "My name is Darcy Andrews, and I'm the panel coordinator here in the CJC. What this means is that I'm going to help you through this process.

"Mrs. Meyer, you said on the phone that you're hoping to move forward with this as quickly as possible, and I think, given the extremely public nature of this incident, that's a good idea. We can show the community that something is being done to help repair the harm. At least the fire was contained to the park!"

She smiles around at us. None of us smile back, though Mom gives a halfhearted shrug of her lips.

Ms. Andrews turns to me. "Gabe, your mom told me that you're ready to take responsibility for your part in Friday's fire."

Wait, what?

Mom grabs my hand. "He is."

Ms. Andrews glances at the hand. "You know what? Mr. and Mrs. Meyer, would you mind waiting in the lobby? I'd love to chat a little with Gabe, and then we can bring you back in."

"Should he have a lawyer?" Dad asks, sounding less like he cares about me and more like he doesn't want to be cut out of the action.

Ms. Andrews shakes her head. "Everything we do here is

confidential, Gabe," she says to me. "Anything we talk about stays right in this room."

My parents look at each other, then, sighing, step out.

As the door closes, Ms. Andrews seems to relax. "So, Gabe, how are you?"

The question catches me off guard. "I don't know," I say. "Not great."

She smiles. "Listen, are we maybe moving too fast with this? Your mom told me that *you* wanted to move forward as quickly as possible, but it seems to me like it's your parents who are ready to move through the process. However, this can't come from them. This whole thing only works if *you* are committed to it."

I dig my toes into the soles of my shoes. She's the first person who's actually asked me how I feel about any of this.

"It's just crazy," I say. "I was fooling around and then there were cops everywhere and my parents are freaking out."

Ms. Andrews nods. "I get it. How about we start at the beginning?"

"Like when I was born?"

She laughs. "If that's where you want to start."

I shake my head, kind of laugh. This lady's maybe all right. So I tell her. Why not? It's all "confidential" she said, which means it's our secret. She lets me talk, asks for more details a few times.

"And then there were fire trucks and flames everywhere," I say. "The cop made out like I meant to burn the whole world." Is it weird that my heart's racing and I'm kind of sweaty?

"But you meant to set off the fireworks?" she asks.

Set them off in Taylor's face. I snort a laugh because it sounds so ridiculous now, after everything. "Yeah, I guess."

"And there was a consequence to that—not what you intended, but a consequence, nonetheless. And some people were harmed by that. This place—the community justice center—is only interested in repairing this kind of harm. We're not a court; we're not here to judge you or punish you."

"So they're not sending me to juvie?"

She shakes her head. "Participants are expected to take responsibility for their actions and acknowledge that justice requires that they do something to help fix the pain they've caused to both individuals and the East Burlington community. We bring together the people who were affected by the crime and the person or people responsible, and together come up with a plan to fix that harm. The plan is called a contract. If the responsible person completes the plan, the case is dismissed and won't show up in any criminal record search."

"What's in the contract?" I ask.

"The contract is whatever the responsible party and the panel come up with. This whole process is about looking at the community as a system, a system that somehow broke down and led to this crime."

"There was no system breakdown," I say, kicking the rug. "I'm just a bad seed."

"Bad to the bone, eh?" She raises her eyebrows.

I snort another laugh. "Everyone thinks it."

She shrugs. "You might be surprised by your community. People are hurt, maybe even angry, but there's something about coming together and talking it through that can really change people's views of things.

"Do you think you're ready to talk with them and start trying to fix this?"

I dig my toes deeper into the soles, practically into the rug. I mean, why delay things?

"Yeah," I say. "Okay."

nine
Rill

THE MORNING LIGHT SLICES into my hollow. I lift my snout, taste the air—my nose smells nothing but smoke and ash. But the air is clean on my tongue. The fire must be far off or dead.

Dead. My thoughts run to my family. I didn't hear them, didn't hear anything but the rush and roar of the flames all night. I should be dead, and I'm more of a coyote than any of my siblings. What chance did those fuzz-heads have? But Mother? Father? It can't be that they're all gone. That I'm alone.

I hear Father's final howl in my mind: *Fern! Pebble! Birch! Sand!* He did not call for me. They are not my pack. Not anymore. So no matter what, I am alone.

I pull my paws under my body and try to stand. A yelp escapes my jaws—the pain is unbearable. My paw pads are raw and red and hurt like teeth scraping across my tongue. I lick my paws, but that only makes them hurt more.

I can't stand. I can't run.

Panic sets my heart racing. The rock walls of this small crevice are dry. The dirt beneath me is damp, but there's not a drop for me to drink. And the forest is quiet, like every other animal has fled for the hills. What will I eat?

I scent the air again, trying to clear my snout of the smoke, of the flakes of ash I can feel blocking my senses. But I get nothing. The air is just smoke and steam and wisps of half-burned leaves.

But there—a dampness. There's a crevice under the ledge, just behind me. I could sneak under the rock—maybe there's water! I drag my body around, paws screaming, then dig out some dirt, making a hole big enough for me to slip into. I can just fit beneath the rock and at the back—water! Just a thin sheen, a few licks and it's gone, but it's something. And it is cool under the rock, which feels good on my burned paws and fur.

A bug scuttles by and I snap it up. So much for a hearty breakfast. That could be it for the day: three licks of dew and a beetle.

I survived the fire, but how will I survive the after?

Ten
Gabe

I STAYED HOME FROM SCHOOL today. I was ready with a fake stomachache, but Mom and Dad were like, *You're staying home and doing this,* then handed me this intake worksheet from the justice center. Ms. Andrews wants to meet with me again, privately. She told me yesterday to have a proposed list of participants by our meeting so she can begin calling people for my panel.

The worksheet is so random. *When things are tough, what kinds of things get you through the tough times?* I skip to the part I know I have to do: the crime stuff.

What did you do? I scrawl in, *Started a fire on accident.*

What were you feeling at the time? Uh, weird question. Okay, um, I was scared of the fire so I write, *Scared.*

Who has been affected by your actions?

The only name I can think to write is mine.

Who else was affected, really? I mean, the fire burned down a portion of a park that's mostly just scrubby trees and rocks. It wasn't the prettiest park to begin with. For real, people only go to Rockledge for the beach. They won't miss the trees. And maybe this will help with the tick situation the park people are always warning the town about. Seriously, it could really be that I'm the only person who's negatively impacted by this whole thing.

I mean, if we change the list to People Who Should Also Be Facing a Community Justice Panel, I can think of two names right away: Owen Shultz and Leo Hilliard. And that Taylor guy. Three names. Boom.

I should totally tell on them.

I toss the worksheet off my bed and roll over, facing the wall. Snitches get stitches, that's the rule, right? What kind of loser would I look like, pointing fingers at other people? Plus, Taylor basically threatened to beat me up if I told on him. Would Leo join in the beating? Would Owen?

I have to squeeze my eyes shut because I WILL NOT BE HURT BY THEM.

Anyway, it's not like anyone would listen to me. The cops wouldn't let me talk before, why would they now? And even if they did, why would they believe me?

I should have run with them when I had the chance.

So I'm back to just the one name: mine. But that's not what the parental units want to see on the list. That's not who Ms. Andrews is looking for.

Fine. Let's write *their* list.

I put down, *People who liked Rockledge Park for the trees.* Okay. There's one. Um, I stole stuff—garbage fireworks that were 80 percent off, but whatever. So there's another person: *Guy who owns the gas station mini-mart.* Um, maybe also, *Clerk at the mini-mart who was too out of it to notice I had stolen the fireworks.* I erase the last part, leave it at *Clerk at the mini-mart.* I can keep that little bit to myself.

Okay, more names. Uh, the fire made a lot of smoke. Maybe: *People who were affected by the smoke from the fire.* And there are houses around the park. Let's add, *People who live near the park.* My parents seemed excited about being included, so I write, *Mom and Dad,* then throw in, *Liz,* since she was all freaked out.

Onto the next question: *What do you think you need to do to make things right?*

This is the whole point of the process, Ms. Andrews said. The plan, how to fix things. I guess I can pay for the fireworks, but the fire? There's no fixing that. It's not like you can rebuild a forest. The truth is, there is nothing I can do to make things right. And if I can't fix the biggest part of this, then is there even a point to this process? There is no way to repair the harm to the community, no way any of the people on this worksheet will ever forgive me.

So there it is. This whole process is a joke. That park is going to be a burned scar for years. And I'm always going to be the kid who did that. The bad kid.

But I need to write something on the form, so I write, *Pay for the fireworks and do something to fix the park.* It's vague enough to hide the truth.

I slide the paper under my door, then flop onto my bed, stick my headphones in, and play video games on my phone.

~

I don't bother asking my dad for a ride to the meeting, I just get on my bike and pedal myself over. There's no one in the lobby again. Is this place always a ghost town, or do they clear it out whenever one of their delinquents is going to show up so the regular people don't have to mingle with the bad guys?

I peek in the cutout and see Ms. Andrews coming down the hallway. "Hey!" she says, waving.

The door buzzes and I open it. "Hi," I say.

"Come in," she says, and leads me down the hall in the opposite direction, toward a corner office that is basically wall-to-wall plants. "Have a seat," she says, pointing to one chair. "Do you have your list?"

I hold out the paper. I'm a little embarrassed. I definitely did it wrong.

"This looks like a great start," she says instead. "I think you're right to keep the list of impacted parties pretty broad. Given the number of people, we'll organize a conference, which will allow for the bigger group."

The word "conference" gets the sweat flowing. "I thought I was doing a youth panel."

"A conference is similar, only instead of being led by the volunteer panelists, the process will be led by one of our staff members.

"I want to talk to you about your role in the process a little more. Part of what you're going to have to do at the meeting is explain what exactly happened before the fire. You did a great job yesterday with starting to put words to your thoughts and feelings. I wonder if we can expand on any of that today. Like here." She points to the paper. "You say you were scared. Were you scared before the fire or because of it?"

All the plants in the office glare at me like they know I'm a tree killer. "It was an accident," I say to them, to her.

"But you told me yesterday that you meant to shoot the fire-works at the dry grass."

Yeah, but I only meant to burn Taylor. I'm not saying that. What else can I say? I start picking this fuzz on my jeans. "I had these friends with me," I add finally. "And they were being really annoying."

"So you were angry with your friends?"

"I didn't say angry," I snap, and then stop because, whoa, why am I angry right now?

Ms. Andrews's eyebrows rise, and she kind of leans into her jungle of plants like they're backing her up on this meeting. "You seem a little angry now."

"I'm not angry, I'm just—" I stop before I call her annoying. "I'm not angry," I say finally.

She takes a breath, puts down her pen. "Look, Gabe, anger isn't anything to be ashamed of. It's just a feeling. We all get angry. What I need from you is to really look inside and find all the feelings you have about this and be honest about them."

"Or I'll end up in more trouble than I'm in now?" I ask, because like, how much worse can it get?

"Gabe, you're not in trouble now," she says. "This process is not about calling you out or making you feel bad. It's about creating a space for you to make things right. Assuming you want to make things right."

"What? I signed the paper."

"You did," she says. "But it's not just a piece of paper. It's an agreement to participate in this process." She tents her fingers over the paper I gave her. "We're trying to do more than just figure out what happened in the park and what you need to do to fix it. We are inviting both you and community members to share your feelings about what happened. I'm sure some of them will be angry, too. But anger isn't the end; it's where we start to look for solutions."

I stare at the fuzz on my jeans and pick at it and pick at it, and this whole string pops out. I bet I've ruined these jeans and they are my favorite jeans, and that is just a perfect thing to happen because I ruin everything.

"Does that make sense, Gabe?"

I nod.

Ms. Andrews smiles. "I need to contact some of the other parties who might want to participate in the conference. Why don't you work on writing more details at home tonight? We can review your notes before the meeting."

I nod. I stand.

"You should also think about who you'd like to have as a support person at the conference with you."

"My parents will be there."

"They're welcome to participate; however, you can choose anyone you want as a support person."

I run a quick check through my life and come up with a big fat no one who supports me right now. Except maybe her.

She holds out her hand to me. "I invite you to take this seriously, Gabe, and to take yourself and your feelings seriously. It's a powerful thing to participate in a panel."

Yeah, but what if all your feelings are bad? I want to ask her, but instead I take her hand. Shake it. "Bye," I say.

I see myself out.

~

I eat granola bars and play video games in bed for the rest of the day. At dinner, Mom knocks and tells me I'm coming downstairs to eat.

"I don't feel good," I yell through the closed door.

"Come down anyway."

"Fine," I say, adding a loud sigh. I stretch, then trudge downstairs making as much noise stomping as possible.

The rest of the family is already sitting at the table. Dinner is pulled pork sandwiches. One of my favorites.

"You waiting to say a prayer or something?" I ask.

"We're waiting for you, dummy," Liz snaps.

"Liz," Dad growls.

She rolls her eyes.

I'm *so* glad that I came downstairs for this.

"Gabe," Mom says like she's beginning a business meeting, "we want you to know that we're proud of you for taking responsibility for your actions and agreeing to participate in this restorative justice program."

Is she reading from one of the justice center pamphlets, because I swear I think one of them says this word for word.

Mom takes a deep breath. "We were hoping you might want to say something to us."

They all look at me. I look back at them. The fridge turns on, whirring noisily.

"What do you want me to say?" I ask finally.

Liz's eyes widen like, *OMG*. Dad tosses his napkin onto the table, a disgusted look on his face. Mom lowers her eyes to her wineglass like, *Give me strength*, and I just say again, "Seriously, what?"

"Gabe, please," Mom says before Dad interrupts.

"Jude, if he doesn't know, he doesn't know. That's it." Dad grabs a bun, forks some pork into it, and takes a huge bite.

Mom sighs. Then she grabs a bun. Liz glares at me. She begins eating.

What did I do? They force me to come down here, then act like I wanted to say something to them—this was just a test made for me to fail.

Mom makes me a sandwich and puts it on my plate. Dinner goes on in silence. I try to take a bite, but I feel sick. I force myself to eat anyway.

When the rest of them finish eating, Liz goes up to her room, Dad heads downstairs to the rec room, turns on the news. Mom starts washing dishes. I just sit there, waiting for . . . I don't know. Some sign that this isn't the rest of my life. Like every moment isn't going to be some test I'm set up to fail. All because of this stupid accident. All because one mistake got so big no one could pretend it wasn't there.

~

I'm woken in the morning by a fist pounding my door. "You're going to school," Mom's voice barks.

I roll over, face the wall.

"GET UP!" she shouts again.

The shouting feels like fists, but I am not going to be hurt by this, NOT ONE BIT, so I sit up, face the door. Mom's shoved a pamphlet under it. *Your Community Justice Panel.* I rip it in half and shove it in the trash.

I put on whatever clothes I can find, and then just grab my coat and walk out the front door. Ride my bike away from the house, away from everything. I end up at school anyway—I'm hungry and it's the only place I can charge a meal; I left the house without my wallet, without my phone even. Digging in my pockets, the only thing I find is another copy of the stupid pamphlet. Mom is cunning.

After scarfing a bagel, I walk to homeroom, just so my name has been checked in. I hide inside my hoodie until the bell rings for first period, then I sneak down to my little place under the stairwell and curl up to sleep.

"Mr. Meyer?" It's my math teacher, Mrs. Dooley. She's one

of those older teachers who wear cardigans and clunky shoes and are big into "classroom etiquette."

"Oh, uh, yes?"

"May I ask why you are sleeping with the dust bunnies under the stairs?"

"Um, uh." My brain is nonfunctional.

"Perhaps we should check in with the nurse?" She pushes her glasses up her nose, the better to glare down at me.

"No, uh, I'm fine, really." If I go to the nurse, they'll call my mom, and like she's going to have any sympathy.

"Gabriel, you do not look fine."

I push my body onto my knees, crawl forward until I can stand. "Seriously, Mrs. Dooley, I was just, uh, tired. Um, I'm going to class."

She looks me up and down. "Perhaps you should stop in the boys' room and"—she waves a hand in the direction of my clothes—"clean yourself up?"

I am covered in dirt and little poofs of . . . I don't want to know what. "Uh, yeah. Good idea."

She nods like she's solved this problem, then follows me to the nearest boys' room, I guess to make sure I actually go. I turn on the sink, splash some water around, until I hear her clunky shoes *tap-tap-tap* away down the hall. Then I lock myself into a stall. This is a quiet end of the school, and it's one of the bathrooms that wasn't remodeled last time around, so hardly anyone comes in here. I tuck my feet up onto the seat, lean my head against the cool tiles. I kind of sleep, kind of don't—the bells go off, announcements bleep out across the air. But I manage to eat the whole school day.

Which means I only have to bike over to the justice center and survive this panel thing, and this nightmare day will be over.

~

There are a bunch of cars in the parking lot. Ms. Andrews must have found a lot of people who wanted to participate. I almost turn my bike around. But then I see Dad's car pulling in. Guess there's no escaping now.

"Let's go," Dad yells to me when he gets out of the car. Liz and Mom stare at me. I walk my bike to the stand and lock it, then follow them inside.

This guy with gray hair and a Santa Claus smile meets us in the waiting room and takes us to the small chair-circle room we were in Monday. "Gabe, you and your support people can wait here," he says, and closes the door.

Support people? From the looks on their faces, boy, is he wrong.

"Sit here, Gabe," Mom says, pointing to a specific chair.

I sit in a different one opposite the three of them. "You didn't have to come," I say.

"This is serious, Gabriel," Dad snarls. "You had better start acting like it. You know what's on the other side of this if you don't do it, right? The juvenile court. Maybe adult court—who knows?"

"Stop, Joe," Mom hisses, "you're scaring him."

No, he isn't. My scared meter went through the roof when I saw the parking lot.

"Well, it *is* the truth," Liz says, gnawing on a cuticle.

No, the truth is I'm about to get eaten alive by a bunch of angry park lovers. The truth is that there's no fixing anything I did. There's no repairing this harm. These people hate me. My family hates me.

There's a knock at the door. Ms. Andrews slips into the room. "We're ready to get started. We'll begin with some informal introductions, and then, Gabe, we'll let you tell your story. Does this all sound okay?" She looks at me and me alone.

"Yes," I say, lowering my eyes like I assume she wants.

"Did you want to go over any of your notes?"

I didn't write any, so no, I don't say. Instead, I just shake my head, like maybe I have notes but don't need to review them. Why take notes when it doesn't matter what I say?

I glance up and see Ms. Andrews squint a little, like she's trying to see through my act. I snap my eyes closed. Which I know is dumb, I mean, it's not like she can read my mind or anything, but I don't want to mess this up. I have to act sad, guilty, ready for change, or whatever else that pamphlet Mom shoved under my door said.

Ms. Andrews leads us down the hall to a door marked PANEL. The noise of voices jumps: the room is filled with people in chairs set in a circle against the walls. Ms. Andrews pats my shoulder, holds the door open for me, and then walks me over to an empty chair.

"Sit down, Gabe," Mom whispers as she sits next to my chair. My butt drops.

Ms. Andrews sits beside me, and Santa sits next to her. The rest of the circle is just a sea of angry eyes.

Santa raises his hand. "I'd like to welcome you all to this panel to address the recent fire at Rockledge Park. Let's start by introducing ourselves. I'm Kevin Darling, I work here at the center, and I have a pug named Henry Higgins."

That gets a few nervous laughs. I can't help but smile picturing a bug-eyed dog in a bow tie.

Each person in the circle introduces themselves. There are doctors, teachers, grocery clerks, construction workers, a trucker, moms, dads, grandparents, and dog, cat, fish, and hamster owners. The circle comes around to me.

Every part of me starts to sweat.

"I'm Gabe," I manage to squawk. "I'm in seventh grade at East Burlington Junior High."

There's some whispering. One lady looks like she's crying.

"Thank you all for being willing to join us today," Santa says. "We're all here to help come up with a plan for how to repair the harm caused by the fire in Rockledge Park last Friday night. We have some ground rules for this process: As we discussed, we're not here to blame or punish anyone. We're here to find a way forward together. Everything we do here is confidential, and everyone's thoughts and feelings are valuable. Our goals today are to deepen our understanding of what happened last Friday, to encourage accountability, to provide an opportunity to heal the community, and to come up with a plan to continue the healing process." He turns to me. "Gabe, I'd like to let you tell us what happened last Friday."

"Um, well," I begin. "I lit a firework and it started a fire."

Santa's eyebrows lift. He glances at Ms. Andrews, who says, "Please, Gabe, try to give us some more details from that evening. Maybe start with where you were before that and what you were doing there?"

I'm already doing this wrong. "Okay, well, I was hanging out with some guys. And we were kind of getting bored—or, I was getting bored, so I went into this mini-mart at the gas station across the street. I was just going for a drink, but then I saw the fireworks, and I was like, *These would be so great,* and they were, like, 80 percent off, but I could only buy them if I was eighteen. So I took a couple. Not just for me, but for my friends. And then we went to the park because it's kind of isolated and dark. I didn't think it was a big deal, just some leftover fireworks. One of my friends—not really my friend—he was bugging me all afternoon, and I thought, just as a joke, I would shoot a firework at him. But then there was a spark in some leaves. I tried to put it out with my jacket. But it got so big so fast."

My heart is racing. My palms are so sweaty, they slide around on my lap. *Stop it,* I think, like telling myself this can stop anything. *Stop, stop, stop.*

"How do you feel about the incident now?" Santa asks.

Like I did it and now I've ruined this park that all these people care about and everyone hates me for it, and there's nothing I can do about it so why are we even here? But I say, "I feel bad."

More murmurs from the crowd.

Santa clears his throat. "Now we're going to let members of the community come forward and speak to you, Gabriel, about the impact your actions have had."

"Sit up straight," Mom hisses.

Thank you, Mom. That little nip from her, from my family, who is so obviously here not to support me but to join in the roast, helps me to refocus. This process is all for show. I just have to get through it.

The first guy to speak is Donald Davis. He owns the mini-mart where I got the fireworks. "Shoplifting has a real impact, son. My business—any small business—is really hurt by even a small theft." It's a little much to call grabbing some old fireworks from the please-take-them sale bin at the back of the store "shoplifting," and it's not like I would have taken them except for the fact that you had to be eighteen to buy them. But Ms. Andrews had said something about "shoplifting," so I guess everyone's jumping on the term.

Next, some guy from the Parks Department talks about the beauty of Rockledge. How the fire damaged "fragile ecosystems." He's calling scrubby pine trees and rocks an ecosystem? "The fire also impacted wildlife. During a wildfire, deer can be chased out into traffic, mothers will flee their nests, leaving behind their babies." All I saw in that park were some squirrels, and I wouldn't exactly call them "wildlife."

This family says their kid got bitten by a coyote the night of the fire. "It just came running out of the woods and attacked our daughter." But wait, they just said that their house was nowhere near the fire. How is this even related?

"We have a team out looking for the coyote," the Parks guy chimes in. "We're going to have to put the animal down."

He says it like this is also my fault. No way. I am not going to feel guilty about some random dog biting some kid just because it happened on the same night.

A bunch of people who live around Rockledge Park start in: "The smoke from the fire blocked out the stars." That could have been a cloud. "The smoke and ash made my asthma act up and I couldn't breathe." It's not my fault she has asthma. "I was driving home from work and could see the flames from the highway." Not possible—no way the fire was that big, right? I mean, the highway's like a mile away . . . "I was afraid my house would burn down." But no house did, so like, calm down, guy.

A parade of people who love Rockledge Park follow: "I walked in Rockledge Park every morning, and now it's all gone." All gone? "My kids grew up playing in Rockledge Park, and now all those memories have gone up in smoke." I didn't burn your memories. "I moved to that neighborhood to be near Rockledge, but now it's just this horrible charred mess." Charred mess? Are we talking about the same fire?

Some small part of me feels the urge to find a phone, check all those news stories I didn't look at. These people are making like this was some huge thing. But it wasn't. It was just in one part of the park. It was a stupid firework. An accident.

"Mr. and Mrs. Meyer?" Santa says. "Would you like to say something?"

"Well, uh, hello," Mom begins, "I think we'd all like to start by apologizing—"

"Mrs. Meyer," Santa says, "how has this fire impacted you?"

Mom runs a nervous finger through her hair. "Well, we've been having a pretty rough year already without this. Joe lost his job in the spring, and I was the first one of us to find full-time work—Joe's been picking up some shifts, but the changes have been hard on the whole family."

That's an understatement.

"And then, to add having to pick up your child at the police station, to see the news and know that they're talking about your kid. It was a lot. It's added a lot."

Mom sounds like she's ready to cry. No, stop. This is really not a part of this.

"I had to cancel a job interview to be here today," Dad says. "I rescheduled, but it doesn't make a good impression to have to reschedule an interview."

I didn't ask him to be here. Why is this my fault?

Then Liz chimes in with, "I have lost so much study time for my exams, if I get terrible scores, it's on you."

"As a reminder," Santa says, "our goal today is not to blame, but to understand and then look forward."

I'd rather everyone do what Liz did. Get things out in the open, honest as the punch to the gut these people all seem to want to give me.

Santa pulls out a paper on a clipboard. "Thank you all for sharing. Now, I'd like to start brainstorming some ideas for how we can begin to repair the harm that you all just described. Gabe, would you like to start?"

No, I think but instead say, "I can pay for the fireworks."

"Great," Santa says. "Restitution is a perfect place to begin." *Begin?* I wait for rotten vegetables to be thrown. But instead, people talk about wanting their park back and whether they can help. They ask that I be given an opportunity to be a part of that rebuilding effort, and they wonder whether the town should start a youth group to provide a place for kids who aren't involved in or can't afford existing programs. I keep waiting for someone to yell, but no one does. In the end, Santa sculpts the group's freewheeling ideas into a few concrete requirements: I have to repay Mr. Davis for the fireworks I stole. And I have to do forty hours of community service repairing the park.

"At one hour per day after school, every weekday," Santa says, "that brings us back here in two months for your review panel. Does this sound agreeable to you, Gabriel?"

Like I have a choice. But then I scan the room and see all these people who didn't yell or throw tomatoes, who seem to almost care about what happens to me, and I kind of want to agree for real.

"Yes, sir," I say.

Ms. Andrews smiles at me.

Santa scribbles his name on the paper, then passes it to Ms. Andrews to sign. She hands it to me.

"Go on, Gabe," Mom says, her voice more sad than angry.

I take the pen. I sign. Then my parents sign.

Santa thanks everyone for coming to the panel and for sharing their stories. He invites them all to come back for the review meeting in two months.

Ms. Andrews leads me and my parents and Liz back to the little room down the hall and hands me a folder. "Here's the information about the restitution and how it can be paid. A notice will follow with the amount," she says. "It also has the contact information for your supervisor with the Parks Department for your community service and a copy of the contract." It's the first time in this whole process things have been handed directly to me, not to my parents.

"I'm proud of you for taking this panel seriously, Gabe. If you continue to engage with this process, I promise you, it works."

We leave out a side door to avoid the crowd in the lobby. It's started to rain, so I can't ride my bike home. Dad shoves it into the back of the minivan. In my seat, I rest my head against the glass and see a couple of people from the panel crying and hugging in the parking lot like they've just left a funeral. Like the fire took away something more to them than just a couple of trees. Suddenly, like a hunger, I need to see what these people are so upset about.

"Can we drive by the park?" I ask as my dad gets into the car.

He and my mom look at each other, then he turns onto the street going toward the lake.

As we drive, I flip through the folder. I have to have the supervisor guy sign off on each day of my community service. I have to get a cashier's check for paying off my restitution. And there, at the bottom of the contract, is the warning: If I don't do it all and do it right, they can bring real charges against me for this. I'd go to court. I'd be a criminal.

The car stops. "Here we are," Dad says.

I look out the window. It's all black. Dead trees, charred black, some standing, some leaning like sticks, some in piles on the black ground. Steam rises up from still-smoldering heaps.

I am a criminal.

"Can we go home now?" I say because the smoke is hurting my eyes and I don't want to see this, I don't want to see this.

"Dad," Liz says, as if she cares about me.

The car backs up, pulls onto the road. We drive to the house in silence. I push through the door and am up the stairs and into my room before anyone else can say another word. I sit in the corner. Feel the wall solid and hard as rock behind my back. And I can finally breathe again.

How could so much have burned?

I find my phone. I search "Rockledge Fire Vermont." I watch all the news footage. I read every article.

But it was just an accident. It was just a stupid accident . . .

eleven
Rill

PEBBLE, IS THAT YOU? MOTHER? Father?

No. Not them.

Noise, rustling from above. Danger?

My body shivers. It's cold and dark and tight under the rock. I can't get out. Everything hurts.

The noise is rain. Little drips hit the stone in front of me, become tiny rivers. My mouth is so dry, I can barely open it to lap up a drop. But I do. I lick every drip, every drizzle. The rain falls harder and a waterfall rushes toward me. It's cool and feels lovely on my whole body. I drink and drink.

As the water spreads through me, I come back into myself. I can sense the different parts of me, not just a cloud of hurt. My paws are points of pain. My fur, patches of dull throbbing. I need to groom those patches, must try to lick my paws to make them stop hurting. But this crevice is too small. I can barely lift my head.

I try to pull myself out from this hole I dug myself into, but I am too weak.

I let my head fall onto the moss. I am stuck. I cannot survive on my own.

My only chance is that my family survived, that somehow they escaped, that they've returned to the forest—I open my jowls to bay, "Father! Mother!" but the howl gets caught in my dry throat and barely echoes around this crevice.

I have to wait, to hope. There's nothing else to do.

TWELVE

Gabe

I WATCHED THEM ALL. EVERY news clip, the live heli-
copter footage, all the interviews. The fire burned eighty-five
acres. Hundreds of trees and shrubs. This giant old monster
of a pine tree, like hundreds of years old, so big it had a name
— the Wolf Tree — went up like a match. The fire even burned
underground, through the roots. A forester said it would never
be the same park. Some guy's chicken coop burned. They think
hundreds of animals might have died — maybe deer, but certainly birds, rodents, skunks, opossums. Maybe even that coyote
who bit the kid, one game warden speculated. One of the later
clips mentions "a local boy" who was found at the scene. In the
clip, a guy who lives near the park said, "I hope they put this kid
in jail."

There's a knock on my door. "Breakfast, Gabe." It's Mom.

I cannot do school today.

"You can't miss school," she says, like she's a mind reader. "It's in the contract."

Contract—what a joke. The news clips make clear that there's no repairing the harm I caused. The place is ruined, forever. But I guess we all signed the "contract," so we all have to pretend . . .

Breakfast is eerily silent. Mom stands near the sink drinking coffee. Dad is rattling around in the garage. Liz sits eating egg whites and toast, lost in whatever's pumping into her earbuds.

"You want eggs?" Mom asks.

"It's okay." I open the pantry. Mom bought my cereal. Two boxes. When did she have time to do that?

"It's not a big deal. I already made your sister some."

"I'm fine." I grab the box and have to walk toward her to get a bowl.

She opens the cabinet and hands it to me. "No one at school is involved in this justice panel stuff, Gabe."

I take the bowl, dig out a spoon, and go for the milk. "It was all over the news, Mom."

"Not your name, nothing about you." She says it like she's trying to make herself feel better. "Just go through your normal day."

Apparently, Mom has forgotten that school is like an information superhighway. You can't tell someone a secret in homeroom and not expect that it won't be an internet meme by lunchtime. So for sure, everyone at school knows about the fire and knows I started it.

At school, the only *good* thing now is that none of my friends are in my house. I never see anyone I know, definitely never run into Owen, Leo, or Taylor. Not that they would come near me if I did. Owen and Leo still haven't sent me one text. Not one email. Nothing. I guess that's what I am to them: nothing.

At lunch, I hide in my dust-bunny cave under the stairs and eat the sandwich Mom made for me. When she handed me the lunch sack, I practically fell over. She even put a note in it: "Have a great day."

The warning bell chimes, so I crush everything into my lunch bag and run for the bathroom. I use a stall because I'm trying to have as little contact as possible with everyone, even in bathrooms. Just as I'm about to step out, the door squeals open and two guys come in.

"I heard he was arrested, like, at the fire."

"Caught with fireworks in his pants," the other guy says, voice spluttering over a choked laugh.

"I mean, what idiot lights fireworks in the woods?"

"You think he was trying to burn it down?"

"He's weird," the first guy says. "I mean, have you seen him hunched under that hoodie?"

The second bell rings. They flush, skip the hand wash—nice—and slam the door against the wall as they leave.

My heart is racing. Sweat has prickled out all over my body. They think I meant it. They think I'm weird. And then I realize that I am hunched on this cruddy toilet under my hoodie and they are right, they are right, they are right.

There's this pressure inside me. It's pushing against my skin, my skull, and I just cannot DEAL.

I punch the stall door. My fist hurts. I punch it again. My fist really hurts. But nothing else does. I punch the door again and again and again until the only thing I can feel is my fist, and it aches and burns and throbs and it feels good.

Because I can't feel anything but that.

I'm crying and laughing because it's good to feel just the one thing, to know that one thing is real and true. I am my throbbing fist.

I have to get to class or they'll call the justice people. I go to stand up, but my head feels like it's a million pounds and everything sways.

I think I might have punched a little too hard.

The throbbing takes over all other thought. My fist is kind of puffing up. I slam open the stall and run cold water from the sink over my hand. My skin is starting to go purple under the red. I need ice, but that means going to the nurse's office.

How am I going to explain this?

Thinkthinkthinkthink . . .

I fell. I tripped on the stairs and slammed my hand on the railing. No, the floor. Broke my fall. I was holding a book, so I hit my knuckles.

They'll call Mom. Or Dad. No, that would be terrible. Absolutely not.

I only have one other option.

~

"You want to tell me what happened?" Liz asks the second I open the car door.

I had to make up a story about my parents having an important meeting with a financial person to get the nurse to call Liz. She's driving Dad's car today since he was just going to be home —overheard that at breakfast. And that's the only lucky thing about this whole situation: the nurse said either she could call an ambulance or I could call my parents, and instead she let me call Liz.

"The nurse told me I have to take you to urgent care?" Liz is staring at me like she cannot believe she's related to me.

"I fell," I say, sliding into the front seat.

Her face is a warped sneer of disbelief. I close the door and we start driving.

"You're lucky I had a free period," she says. "You want me to drop you off at home, or what?"

I look down at my hand, which is becoming kind of a purple mess.

"Oh my god," Liz says, slamming on the brakes. "Okay, what happened? Did someone go for you? Did you punch someone?"

"A bathroom stall."

She just kind of stares at me.

"What?" I snap.

She rolls her eyes, shakes her head. "Gabe, what is going on? Your hand looks like it got run over."

"I punched a bathroom stall."

"Why would you punch a bathroom stall?" she asks like she's talking to a crazy guy coming at her with a hammer.

"Because it made everything else hurt less," I say.

She stares at me for another minute, like maybe there's more explanation coming, but there is no explanation. There was this explosion inside me and I had to get it out, and this was how it came out.

"I have Advil and an Ace bandage in my gym bag. And we can steal ice from the coach's office." She pulls out of the parking lot and drives toward the high school.

"You'll help me?"

She wrings the steering wheel with her fists. "Someone has to."

We park around the back of the high school, and Liz sneaks me in through the gym door—she has a key because she helps the football team's trainer when she's not at soccer practice; it looks good on a college application, I guess. The locker room is quiet and echoes like a cave.

Liz takes my hand, begins feeling along the bones like she knows something about medicine.

"What are you doing?"

"Making sure you didn't do anything really stupid," she says. "Nothing's broken." She pulls a bandage from her bag and holds the end against my hand. "I'm sorry I freaked out at you." She glances up at me, then back at the bandage.

I don't say anything, don't really want her apology.

Liz finishes wrapping my hand, then hands me an ice pack. "Do you want me to take you back to school?"

Liz did a decent job on the wrap. "Thank you," I say.

"Yeah, well, you're not having the best week. I'll give you this one pass."

I check my phone. It's close enough to 2:30 and I don't think I can ride my bike right now—it can spend one night at school. "Can you drop me off near the park?" It's probably not a good idea to skip out on the first day of community service, even if I have a possibly broken hand.

~

Liz drops me off near the sign at the entrance to Rockledge Park. The sign is unburned, though the grass all around is trampled and the tracks of large wheels have left ruts in the dirt.

There's a closed-up ranger station not far in from the sign. The trees around it are okay. But behind it, there's a clear-cut where they put in a firebreak to protect the houses. And beyond that, just this blackened disaster zone. It still smells like smoke.

A man and a woman in green uniforms with game warden badges walk out of the park. They're talking to each other, ignoring me.

"We'll check the western quarter tomorrow. Griffin thought he saw a den there over the summer. Could be it's hiding there."

"Coyotes are sneaky," the lady responds. "But we'll get this one."

Coyote. Something buzzes in my memory—they mentioned a coyote at my panel. It bit some kid the night of the fire. It has to be put down . . . Put down, like dead?

Not my fault. But still . . .

"Hey there!" a guy shouts from behind me. I turn and there's this twenty-something guy in a tan jumpsuit. "I'm guessing you're Gabe? Zach Donahue." He's the forester from the news clip.

Zach's not much taller than me and has this thatch of reddish-brown hair that sticks up all over the place. His cheeks are red like he's been running, but he's not sweaty—maybe that's just his face? He's carrying a rake, wears a work belt that looks like armor, it's got so many carabiners and tools hanging off it, and shoulders a backpack full of stuff studded with even more carabiners.

"Quite a mess you've made here, kid," he says. "Let's get in there and see what can be done."

And that's it. No lecture. He just walks into the park and keeps going. I kind of stand there for a minute, waiting for a better explanation of what exactly he means for me to get "done," but he just plows ahead, and so I have to run to catch up with him in the clear-cut.

"Your shoes are going to be a problem," he says, still walking. "You have hiking boots? Anything made of leather with a thick sole?"

My sneakers are not in great shape, but it's this or some black dress loafers my mom got me for my class service at Hebrew school last year. "I guess I could get some," I say, trying to estimate how much leather shoes cost.

"So that's a no," Zach says, stepping over a burned log. He stops, slips off the pack, and pulls out a pair of old boots. He squints at my feet, squints at the boots. "Should work," he says, and then tosses them at my chest. I fumble them but manage to hug the boots to me.

"You want me to put these on?" I ask.

"You want to melt your sneakers and possibly burn off your feet stepping on the wrong pile of ash?"

"No," I whisper to myself, already tugging my shoes off and jamming my feet into what I guess are his old boots. Either he assumed I was clueless—which I guess I am—or that pack is just full of boots. The ones he gave me are a little big, but better than the possibility of melting and burning. I shove my sneakers into my backpack and race after him.

"This whole ridge is going to be an issue," he says. He reaches down, pinches the dirt. "You can already see that the little sprinkle we got yesterday has caused erosion. We're going to need to put in containment measures, try to keep some of that thin soil up here or we're going to have no trees and problems with lake water quality."

He points to this ledge in front of us, like a half a football field away. "The fire not only took out the vegetation—it fried the soil underneath. You see the lines of dirt? The rain fell on the thin layer of topsoil along that ledge and the dirt is so dry, it's just running off. There are no plants or tree roots to hold it up there. And if it all runs off, then we have nothing for new plants to grow on. And worse, where do you think all that silt ends up? In the lake.

"I'm going to have you help me finish surveying the burned area of the park." He hands me a map. "I already sketched out the boundaries of the fire—basically, it's the firebreak. What I want you to do is to make note of any large piles of brush that you see. We're going to have to clear those out. I want to spread some vermicast, get this soil back to life! Any of those little trails of dirt, mark those, too. You know how to use a compass? Find points on a map?"

I'm just staring at this map with all these squiggly lines and tiny numbers and little handwritten notes scrawled in the corners. "I'm sorry," I say.

Zach shrugs. "I guess we'll start with that."

He snaps a compass off a carabiner, shows me how to use it. He points out north on the map, that north on the compass and north on the map are the same. That the squiggly lines represent the "topography" of the park, or the ups and downs of the ground. I feel like I learn more in fifteen minutes than I've learned in my whole life.

"Go north to the firebreak and start walking back south from there. I'm going to start out by the lake and come east. We'll meet back here and see what we've got."

"Wait, you're not coming with me?"

He looks confused. "Do you need me to come with you?"

I kind of take that in, look at the map, the compass. "No, but—"

"No *but*s," he says, adjusting his pack. "Just do like we talked about, and I'll see you back here in an hour." He hikes off west toward the far lakeshore.

"No *but*s," I whisper to myself, unable to hold back the smile that creeps out on my lips. Then I hold the compass to my belly button, get the red line to match up with north, and follow that through the charred remnants of Rockledge Park until I hit the firebreak.

I start making notes on the map, hoping I'm actually marking the right spots and not messing things up for Zach.

The compass has me climbing up a ledge. It's actually fun —I think Mom took me here once when I was little. All the ledges and moss and trees made it feel like a fairy tale. The rock ledge is different now. The moss is all burned off. The trees are gone or just blackened sticks. And I did this.

This root shoots up out of nowhere, my foot catches, and I'm down. When my arm hits dirt, I drop the compass and it tumbles into a crevice.

Nice one, I tell myself.

I crawl over to the crevice. The compass is at the bottom. At least this crack in the ledge is big enough for me to squeeze into. I slither my legs inside it, then have to kind of crumple down —no way I can bend over. I get into a crouch and can just feel my fingers on the compass when I hear it.

Grrrrrr.

The rock just growled at me.

Grrrrrrrr. Louder now.

I twist my head. Eyes flash in the dim light. There's something down here.

Fingers trembling, I dig for my phone in my backpack, pull it out, hit the flashlight. There's a little ledge where the rock meets the dirt, and the rain maybe washed out a tiny cave under it, and in that ridiculously small cave is a dog.

"What are you doing here, dog?" I whisper.

It growls at me, this time lifting its jowls so I can see its teeth.

The dog's fur is covered in dirt and dust, but I can also see black and raw red. One paw sticks out a little and it looks bad, like this dog ran through the fire. The dog also doesn't look like a regular pet or anything—no collar, and it has a kind of pointy snout and stuck-up ears, like a giant fox-wolf.

Oh, man. This is that coyote, the one that bit the kid. I absolutely bet it is. "They're looking for you," I whisper.

It growls again. But it's not moving, not even its head. Can it get out of there? And how long has it been there? When was the last time it ate?

I drag my backpack over my head, slide it off my arms, and dig for something to feed this guy. There's a little crumb of Power Bar stuck in a wrapper. I pull it out, drop the little bit of food in front of the hole.

The coyote growls again, softer this time. Then it sniffs at the Power Bar. It sticks out its tongue. Tries to move its head but can't. It growls more, then whimpers.

"It's okay, girl," I whisper. It don't know why I say "girl," but whatever—I'm calling it a girl. I find a little stick and shove the morsel closer to her nose.

She growls until I move the stick away, then sniffs again. She sticks her tongue out and manages to lap up the crumb. Her jaws can barely move to chew, but she does it and swallows, then looks at me for more.

"Sorry, girl," I whisper, but then add, "Tomorrow. I'll bring more tomorrow." I pull out my water bottle and pour a little into this depression in the rock near her nose. It'll have to be enough.

"Gabe! You lost?" Zach's calling.

I wriggle myself to standing and yell back over the edge of the crevice, "Coming!" I glance back down at the coyote. Her eyes glint in the darkness. She's watching me. "I'll be back," I tell her.

I pull myself up and out onto the top of the ledge. I mark her location on the map, take a picture of the map with my phone, and then erase the mark. I can't let anyone find her, not even Zach. He works for the town; he probably would have to tell them if he found her. But if anyone else finds her, they'll turn her in. And I can't let that happen. The coyote was clearly in my fire, either running from it or being chased into it. I did this to her. Which means I have to help her get out of trouble.

I run to meet Zach. "Let's see what you've done," he says, not looking up and just holding a hand out. I put my map in his hand. "Uh-huh," he says, looking over it. "Nice job. Well, I'll see you tomorrow."

"I'm done?" I look at my phone. Holy crud, it's been an hour and a half.

"You're done," he says. "Same time, same place tomorrow?"

"Yeah, sure," I say. "See you then." I turn to go, but Zach doesn't follow. "Are you leaving?"

"Nah," he says, marking something on his phone. "I have more of the park to go over."

"Oh, okay," I say. "See ya." I would stay and help, but I have homework, and Mom and Dad will freak if I'm home late. And I should also maybe research what coyotes eat. And maybe something about how to heal burns?

It takes a while to walk home, so by the time I'm there, everyone's already in the house — no escaping upstairs for me.

"You have a notice here concerning your restitution," Mom says when I walk in the door.

I take it from her, read it. "Can I borrow twenty bucks?"

"No, you cannot borrow twenty bucks. You can earn your own money."

"How am I supposed to earn my own money? I have to do community service every day."

"I didn't steal any fireworks. Why should I pay for it?" Mom gives me this look, eyebrows up, head cocked, daring me to talk back.

"Fine," I say, and take the paper up to my room.

They want to make this as hard for me as possible, that's so typical. I kick some junk across my floor. A bottle rolls out from under my bed.

Recycling. We used to do the bottle return at the grocery store together when I was little. I made ten bucks one time. And that was just recycling bottles and cans! Done and done—I can do twenty bucks, easy. Maybe I can even raise some extra money to buy some dog food or something for my coyote.

Huh, weird to call her *my* coyote. But I guess she is, right? I bet I'm the only one who knows where she is, and I'm the only one who can help her.

THIRTEEN

Rill

I CANNOT BELIEVE I ATE the human's food. Did I learn nothing from what happened to Boulder and Maple? Never eat human treats, never.

But I am so hungry.

I battle with myself for the rest of the sun—this is madness; this is survival. Until finally, as the sun is setting, I admit that whatever it is, it is done. The human gave me food and I ate it, and whatever happens to me next is going to happen.

I lie still, waiting for this mystery monster, whatever made Boulder and Maple disappear. At least my human didn't blast any fire sticks.

These terrible thoughts are interrupted by pebbles plinking down and tumbling against my skin. It's happening. Whatever took Maple and Boulder after they ate the human food, it's here.

I close my eyes.

More grinding of stones and shuffling of dirt—strange. I sniff, stretch my head out from under the rock, and am greeted by a strong scent: rodent, but worse. Opening my eyes, I see my stinky visitor—an opossum, all spiny white fur and beady eyes and black ears like mushrooms sticking up from its head.

Is this what took my brothers? No, impossible—but just in case, I growl, and it hisses, baring its pointy little teeth.

"Get out of my den, rat-tail," I snarl, trying to sound more dangerous than I am.

Instead of running away, the thing freezes, eyes wide, fur bristling.

Weird. No scurrying, no running away. So I suck in a deep breath and add as loud as I can bark it, "GET OUT!"

The opossum squeals and flops onto its side. A bubble of snot forms at its nose. Drool drips out of its mouth. It smells terrible. And it doesn't look like it's breathing. *Burrs and prickers* —did I scare the thing to death?

It's just my luck that I scare something remotely edible to death and it's beyond the reach of my jaws and also smells terrible.

Just as I begin to contemplate how much worse the smell has to get before I attempt to drag my broken body out of this hole, the opossum's ear moves. Wait—maybe it's a death jolt. Happens sometimes. But no, look there—the feet are moving and now the nose is twitching, and I cannot believe it but the opossum is not dead at all. Or it was and opossums can die and then come back to life? Now I'm the one who's shaking in her fur.

"Are you—" I begin. "I mean, did you just . . ."

The opossum squeals, whips around, and opens its mouth to hiss and show me all of its many pointy teeth again. So definitely not dead anymore.

"You can stop the show," I yip. "I'm not going to eat you, certainly not after having smelled you."

The hissing stops. The opossum closes its jaw, tilts its head, and considers me with its bulbous black eyes. "Why aren't you trying to eat me? Dogs always try to eat me." It's a male opossum and on the youngish side.

"Not a dog," I woof, skipping over the fact that I am currently stuck in place and couldn't eat him even if I wanted to.

"Then what's this human food doing here?" He picks up a crumb I missed. "Humans feed dogs and cats, and you are not a cat."

"How do you know this is human food?" I growl.

The opossum waves one of his strange humanlike paws— it's pinkish and flattish and has long, hairless toes. "I know my human garbage. And this is human food." He shoves a delicious crumb into his mouth. "*Mmmm-mmm.* I've pulled bites of this out of the trash from the finest human dens."

"I don't go near humans," I snap. "Humans are bad."

The opossum sniffs around. "Not so bad that you won't eat their food. Got any more lying around? I'm having a bit of a tough night scavenging. Whole forest is dead up there."

He says it so casually—*Dead.* The word freezes my heart.

"So, dog, why are you here and not with your human?" The rodent continues poking around my cave. "Shouldn't you be curled up in some bed, snuggling beside your master?" He flashes a sly smile at me over his shoulder.

I will not be taunted by this rodent. "I told you," I growl, "I am NOT A DOG!" I lunge forward, scraping my paws and back on the rocks, and snap my jowls at his hairless tail.

"Hoppin' toad babies!" he squeals. "All right, I'm going, I'm going!" And he scrambles up and out of my crevice.

Only then do I feel the hurt in my body—new pain. I ripped my paws, bruised my fur. Oh, I hurt. I curl back under my rock. Please stop. But then the pain in my body is overshadowed by the pain that blossoms inside, knowing now that the forest is dead and my family with it. Gone, gone, because of me. Because I left them.

Oh, what have I done?

Fourteen

Gabe

IT IS UNBELIEVABLE THE NUMBER of cans you can find by just walking around. Last night, I searched through some scrubby woods near my house and found ten cans just tossed into the leaves. On the way to school—Liz gave me a ride—I saw a bunch more just lying around. I have a trash bag in my backpack so I can snag them all on my way to community service after school.

The bell rings, and I have lunch then recess. No reason not to scan around the school for free money, so I head outside.

I stop on the blacktop to check in the garbage—I cannot skip any sources of can money—and hear these feet *slap, slap* over to me. I look up and Cora Phillips is hovering near me, twisting the toes of her bejeweled sneakers in the dust.

"So, like, everyone's talking about this fire," she begins,

"and I heard that maybe you were there? Like, actually, I heard that you started it?"

It starts as a rumble, like a tiny earthquake inside, somewhere near my navel.

"And that you got arrested? I mean, is that true?"

It stretches up and out, and I feel like my bones are trembling.

"What was it like? Were you in a police car?" She bends her head to look into my face. "Earth to Gabriel?"

Cora's sparkling shoes tell her whole story: huge house meaning big money, over-attentive parents, perfect life. We've been in school together since kindergarten. She's always acted like she's better than everyone else. And here she is questioning me like she's been appointed queen of all seventh-grade gossip.

And then I see Taylor over with Cora's gang of friends, laughing, whispering.

The earthquake is so strong, it rattles my teeth, and all I want to do is make him and her and all of them GO AWAY and—

"AGH!" I scream, and kick the trash can, and it skids into Cora's perfect sneakers, then topples over, launching an avalanche of garbage—including a carton of chocolate milk—straight onto her shirt.

She shrieks, hands up and waving. "Gross!" she says, surveying the calico blobs on her clothes. She runs on tiptoes through the lunchroom doors.

Her gaggle of friends comes bustling over and shuffles in behind her. As one—Ophelia Kirk—passes, she whispers, "Freak." Taylor disappears around a corner.

I'm sweating and shaking and the whole school is staring at me, and I cannot believe I kicked the garbage can. That contract with the justice center said I can't violate any rules. Was that a violation? Please, please, don't let it be a violation. I was doing so good, and it was mostly her fault—I mean, why did she even come over to me? Taylor must have told her everything.

I have to clean it up. Then, maybe, no one will notice. I kick all the trash back into the can and set it upright.

I hear a ball bounce and hope maybe everyone has moved on. I dare to look up. Some kids are still staring, but no lunch monitor approaches. Maybe everything's cool.

Stay cool, stay cool . . .

I march to the field, along the edge of the grass, all the way to the far corner, away from the school, behind the backstop. It's quieter here. I take a deep breath.

It's cool, it's cool . . .

I sit on a wooden bench and spot the glisten of plastic in the sun. Right, recycling. That was my whole purpose in coming out here.

I stand and begin poking through the grass.

Three Gatorade bottles behind the backstop alone! This is a major score. I'll be to twenty bucks in no ti—

"Hey."

I turn around. Owen is standing there. I go back to kicking the tall grass.

He doesn't leave. "What are you doing?"

"Why do you care?" I snap, not looking at him. I grab a dented can.

He doesn't say anything but also doesn't go away. "I saw the news," he says finally.

The rumble starts to expand inside me again, it presses against my stomach, my ribs.

"You okay?" he asks.

I suck in air, breathe it out. *Stay cool, stay cool.* "Fine," I say, and walk toward the fence.

"Hey!" someone shouts from the field. "Owen!"

I keep walking.

"I'll see you," Owen says.

I crouch down like I've spotted something awesome in the shadows beneath a bush. When I look back over my shoulder, Owen is already running onto the field, rejoining the regular kids, the ones who aren't on the news, the ones who never got shoved into a police cruiser or forced to sit through a community justice panel.

I elbow my way between the branches pushing into the darkness of the woods, telling myself I'm looking for recyclables, but really it's just better here, alone, in the dark.

~

After school, I bike over to Rockledge. I pull Zach's old boots on and have them tied just as he pulls up in a beat-up Subaru. He gets out and starts walking, same as yesterday.

"We've got work to do," he yells to me as he passes.

I grab my backpack and follow him.

"We're going to start by dragging all the burned brush into piles. Use the places you marked on your map where there are already piles and add to those. We want as much of the burned, dead stuff cleared out. Then we can start with bringing in vermicast and laying some straw barriers along the ridge to keep the erosion down to a minimum."

"Why are we doing this?" I dare to ask. "The trees are all gone. The place is a dead zone."

"Dude," Zach says, like I'm being ridiculous, "a forest is not just trees." He pulls out a trowel, jams it into the gray dirt, and digs down. "See the layers?" The dirt goes from this skin of gray to crumbly brown to deep brown. "The top layer? That's toasted. These next few inches? Roasted. But down here?" He points to the deep brown. "This is still alive."

"It's just dirt."

"Dirt is not *just* one thing. Dirt is minerals and bacteria and fungi, all of which make trees and plants possible, which make animals and hiking trails possible. It's a system that starts with the invisible and leads to a park. This fire? It's upset the system.

Our job is to bring all the invisible parts of that system back to these roasted and toasted layers so the big parts can grow themselves."

Systems. Everyone's talking about systems. I've never been a part of a system, and now I'm mixed up in the community's system and the dirt's system.

Zach slaps a pair of leather work gloves on the log next to me. "We good?"

"Yeah." I take the gloves.

"Then let's get going."

I pull out my compass and walk to the northern edge of the firebreak, then stop and listen — nothing but some birds, the wind in the leaves. I flip my phone to the picture I took of the map and creep along until I find what I think is the right crack in the rock. I shine my flashlight down. Yep, there's the sparkle of my coyote's eyes.

The game wardens haven't found her. At least, not yet.

"Hey, girl," I whisper.

She growls a hello.

I open my backpack. I "borrowed" some items from home this morning. Online, I did research on healing burns. There's not much to do except try to keep them from becoming infected. I don't have antibiotics, but I did have some triple antibiotic ointment that Mom uses on cuts. One article said you could put socks on a dog's paws if they're burned, and so I also have an old pair of mine that have a hole on the toe. I doubt the coyote will let me touch her at all, but I can try.

To begin, I break a stick of jerky I found in the pantry into bits. I drop one jerky bit down, right in front of her nose. She growls louder, but then sniffs and licks the crumb of meat up.

Along the top edge of the crevice, I line up the rest of the jerky bits, my water bottle, and the top from a giant value-sized peanut butter jar that I rescued from the recycling bin. Then I slide into the hole. Now she's really growling.

"It's okay, girl," I whisper. "I'm here to help you."

I grab a few jerky bits from the top of the ledge, then kneel down and place them in front of her. She grumbles a little and licks the bits up fast. I put a few more down. Just a hint of grumble, then she's lapping up the crumbs. I put the last bits down. She licks them up without even a whimper of noise. Once she's eaten the big pieces, she starts licking at the crumbs. Now's my chance. I shine my phone light into her cave to see her paws. They're stuck beneath her, out of the reach of her jowls, but also out of my reach.

I think about sticking a hand in real quick, just dabbing some ointment on the closest paw and whipping it back out, but the coyote notices me: she stops licking the rock for crumbs and growls at me, even bares her teeth. I am *not* sticking my fingers in there now.

So no ointment, at least not today.

I stand and grab the peanut butter jar lid, fill it with water from my bottle, then kneel back down and slide it in front of her nose. She growls again but not in a serious way, then starts licking at the lid. She spills some but gets the idea that the water is inside the lid and kind of lifts her nose to better lap it up.

"That's my girl," I whisper to her.

She looks at me with this death glare and starts to grumble again.

"Okay," I say, "I get it." I stand and pull myself out of the crevice. Before I go, I check in the hole. She's licking up the water. She liked it. She needs it. She needs me.

I pull on my gloves as I walk back toward the firebreak. There's a lot of brush to move. But I can handle it.

~

Saturday morning, first thing, I pack my backpack with water and granola bars and drag my two garbage bags of cans to the supermarket to recycle them in the machines. In the end, my two big bags gave me only four bucks. And I have to buy more jerky for my secret coyote.

After I go in to cash my slips and buy the stick of jerky, I'm left with one dollar and some change. Saving twenty bucks is going to take forever.

I have to up my recycling game. There were cans all along the scrubby grass bordering the parking lot at Rockledge. I can start there.

It's a little gross, picking up the older cans. Some are covered in dirt and dead leaves, some still have something sloshing around inside them.

After I scavenge the whole lot for cans, it's time to feed my coyote. The park is roped off to visitors, but I'm kind of officially required to go in there. And I have a hungry girl waiting for me.

I walk up to the yellow police tape.

"Hey, kid," some guy yells. "No one's allowed in there."

I turn. It's just some guy walking his dog. "Oh?" I say, like an idiot because what else am I going to tell him? *Hey, it's okay, I'm the kid who burned down your park, and I have to feed my secret coyote so she doesn't die because of the whole "burning her while also burning down the park" thing . . .*

He looks past me at the fringe of trees left on this end of the park. "Yeah, not until they finish cleaning up the damage," he says, then adds, kind of wistfully, patting his dog's head, "We used to walk in there every day."

I don't say anything. He's not telling me because he wants an apology—he has no idea I did this. But it's weird because the first thing that jumps into my head is *I'm sorry*, not, *It was an accident.*

I head toward my bike, wait for him to walk on. When he's far down the road, I check again that the coast is clear, then slip into the trees. It's funny how all the sounds from the road disappear once you cross into the thickness of the leaves. I mean, I can hear the occasional car horn or squeal of tires, but it's mostly just rustling leaves and birdcalls. It's nice. But then I hit the burned part, and it's all just . . . empty. Blackish dirt and sticks. Even the thick carpet of dead leaves is gone.

I climb over some blackened branches I guess I missed on Friday. At first I'm like, whatever, but then I think, I'm going to have to move them Monday, so I just drag them to my big pile. My ungloved hands get covered in ash. Okay, so next time I bring work gloves. I'm sure Dad has some in the garage.

I get to my girl's cave and toss down some jerky. She doesn't even growl. I see her nose poke out of the shadows, and she licks up the crumbs of food. I line up my water bottle and jerky along the edge of the crevice and slide down to her. Now she starts growling, but I take that as a good sign. She's still got fight left in her. I break up the jerky into bits and toss them close to the opening of her cave while also checking for a glimpse of her paws. They're still hidden in the cave, and she's still stuck in the one position.

I find a stick and poke the plastic edge of the jar lid until I manage to flip it away from her and toward me.

That sets off a huge growl and even a little yip from my girl.

"Quiet, now," I tell her like she's some whiny kindergartner. And that makes me smile because she totally is whining.

I've always wanted a dog. Liz and I begged my parents for one back when Liz was in junior high. But they were both like,

Dogs are expensive, and who's going to walk it on those freezing cold winter days? Even though Liz and I were like, *We will, we promise!,* the issue was dead on arrival with my parents. I tried to push it again this summer when Mom revealed she was going back to work, but Liz was like, *I'm too busy for a dog,* and my parents were even more on the dogs-are-expensive bandwagon. I get it now—it's probably not a good idea to take on new expenses when one parent is scrounging for hours at a hardware store —but back then, I was so angry.

I fill the water bowl, make sure the jerky bits are all close enough for her to lick up, and drag myself out of the hole. Packing my water bottle and the wrapper into my backpack, I feel kind of bad about how nasty I got over the whole dog thing. I kind of screamed at my parents. I told them that they didn't need to make up lame excuses when the real reason was they didn't care what *I* needed. Now, thinking about it, even I can see the drama I was working. It's clear that it didn't have so much to do with not wanting to get me a dog, but not being sure about the future.

I'm still not okay with it. But I get it. A little.

~

By Sunday afternoon, I have a pretty big pile of deposit cans and bottles. My legs are like jelly—I had to ride practically from one end of town to the other to collect them all. And I had competition. I saw this guy—a real grownup, like Dad's age

—doing the same thing as me. Is this something grownups do for money? It felt weird competing with him, so I kind of left him the entire east side of the shopping center.

A bunch of the cans are gross—covered in dirt or leaves, dripping mystery liquids. So now I'm camped out on the patio wearing a pair of dish gloves and using the hose to clean them off.

I saved some burger meat from Saturday's dinner to feed my girl this morning. She seemed to like it, so I'm thinking I'll use some of the money to buy ground beef today. If I cook a whole package, I could bring a little bit to her each day during the week. It would be cheaper than the beef jerky sticks.

I'm finishing rinsing an especially funky bottle when I hear someone rattling down the sidewalk. It's Owen, hauling a huge trash bag.

He stops at my fence. "Hey."

I keep rinsing the bottle.

"It's pretty ridiculous to pretend I'm not standing here when I know you saw me."

I make a real show of spraying the bottle with the hose on its highest setting.

"You're not talking to me now? Not at school or here?"

He waits. I scrub.

"Have you read my texts? I even sent you an email."

I have not. And I don't plan to. He waited until yesterday to send anything. It took him three texts to get to *I'm sorry.* Okay, so I read them . . .

"I shouldn't have run," Owen says. "Or I shouldn't have run without making sure we all ran."

No, you shouldn't have. Friends don't do that. Not that you've been my friend for a while. It just took burning down a forest and you and Leo leaving me to get caught for me to finally see it.

"I can't believe they arrested you." He shifts his Santa sack of trash, and there's this clanging music from inside.

Is he bringing his recycling somewhere?

"I mean, it was an accident. I never thought—"

"What do you want, Owen?" I snap. Because I'm not interested in hearing his lame excuse for not turning himself in, for not coming to defend me, for not calling someone to back me up on how this was totally a stupid mistake. For waiting until yesterday to even acknowledge he did anything wrong.

He shifts again, and the sack rattles and chimes. "I asked my parents if I could give you our deposit bottles and cans."

I squint at him—it's not like I told him my plans.

"I saw you picking up cans and stuff at school, and I heard that the police are making you pay restitution—I had to look that up. It's just insane that the news is using, like, official words to talk about you."

"I don't want your cans." I don't need his pity cans. This is the most chicken thing he could do. Does he think this somehow makes up for anything that happened?

"I'm sorry, Gabe." Owen flips the sack over the fence, drops it in my yard. "I messed up. I was scared. I don't know what else to say. It sucks what happened to you—"

"Is happening," I correct. "I'm being punished right now. I don't see you stepping up and taking your forty hours of community service. So don't pretend you're sorry. You just *feel* sorry for *me*. And I don't need that from you or Leo or that jerk Taylor."

Owen taps the fence, like maybe he's going to say something, but apparently he has nothing to say to that. He walks back up the street, silent now, no ringing sack of garbage weighing him down.

I finish the cleaning, count my cans. Maybe four bucks, maybe a little more.

Just because it's there, I check Owen's bag. It's full of already-clean cans and bottles. Another four bucks. Maybe more.

A whole weekend of work.

A part of me is like, *You should have said thank you.* But the rest of me is like, *No way I'm ever thanking him.* This is the bare minimum, the absolute least he could do.

Still, it's nice to have that extra four bucks.

Everyone's sitting down to dinner when I come inside. "Wash your hands," Mom says, bringing a bowl with a steaming pile of something green to the table.

Not even a *Hey, Gabe, how was your weekend of collecting trash?* Just *Wash your hands.*

I do head to the bathroom to wash my hands—not because Mom told me to, but because my hands are gross from having touched all those cans and bottles, even through the gloves. Back at the table, they're talking about something quietly, but then all stop and look at me as I walk into the kitchen.

"What?" I say. I sit, slop green stuff and rice and chicken parts onto my plate.

"Nothing," Mom says. "We were just talking about how proud we are that you're working so hard."

"I don't have a choice, do I?" I poke and poke at a chicken wing and then just pick it up with my fingers.

"Gabe," Dad starts, but Mom flashes him a look.

"This might be a part of the community justice program, but it's still your choice to really take the process seriously and we are proud of you for that."

For some reason, Mom's words feel like she's talking down to me, like I'm some baby who just stopped putting sharp objects in his mouth. I stuff rice and green stuff into my face to keep from saying something that's just going to get me in trouble.

Mom gives Dad another look, this time eyebrows up, like she's prodding him into action.

Dad splutters, swallows, then says, "I see you have a lot of cans out there. How about I give you a ride to the deposit center after school tomorrow?"

Before the summer, Dad barely ever gave me or Liz a ride anywhere—that was Mom's job. After he lost his job and was the more at-home parent, Dad still made us feel like any ride he gave us was a huge deal. No way I'm falling for whatever is going on with this offer.

"I have community service." I chew, swallow.

"After that, then," he says, voice becoming a little more strained. So now he's angry that I'm *not* taking a ride from him? I cannot win with this family.

"Don't worry about it," I say, finishing off my dinner. I stand, taking my plate, silverware, and milk glass with me. "I'm doing this all on my own, remember." I choke down the whole glass of milk, drop the dishes into the sink, and lock myself in my room.

I have a ton of homework to catch up on. It's another part of the contract—it's not only staying out of trouble and finishing the community service and paying the restitution, but I also have to stay in school and keep my grades up.

I'm halfway through math when I hear a knock on my door. "What?" I snap.

"Can I come in?" It's Liz.

I sigh. It's like this family can't stop picking at me like some itchy scab. "Fine," I say, spinning around and opening the door. "What?"

"You could start by checking that attitude," she says, slipping into my room.

"I cannot believe you of all people just said that to me."

She shrugs. "Mom and Dad are trying to engage with you. You don't have to be such a jerk."

"*Engage with me?* They could talk to me like a normal person, but instead they're talking to me like I'm some dangerous criminal."

"They're trying," she says. "It might not be perfect, but they're reaching out."

"Not far enough to give me twenty bucks."

"You can't see how that's different?" she asks.

And I can. Kind of. Like, it'd be one thing to do the community service for me and another to give me a ride to the job site, but still. I'm not in the mood to agree with Liz about this right now. "You done dispensing advice? I have homework."

Now it's her turn to sigh dramatically. "It's not the worst thing in the world to accept help when someone offers it." She lets herself out of my room and closes the door behind her.

I turn back to my math, but the numbers swim on the paper. I wipe my face with my sleeve because I am not some crybaby loser. And I don't need help. I can do this whole community contract thing on my own. Because that's the whole point, right? For me to take responsibility. For me to make up for what I did. Me alone.

Me.

Alone.

I drink some water. Stare at the rug. The tears won't listen to me, and they drip, drip, drip out of my eyes like there's a crack somewhere in the pipes that can't be fixed.

FIFTeeN
Rill

I'M NOT SURE WHAT TO MAKE of this human who keeps leaving tasty bits of meat and water for me. He brings no traps, blasts no fire sticks, and doesn't seem to have any interest in taking me from this cave. He just brings me food and water. Is this human trying to be kind? No—that is not the human way.

Yet, to be entirely nose-to-tail about things, I would not be alive without this human. There hasn't been prey anywhere near my hole in the days I've been trapped here, no real rain, either. My paws feel the slightest bit better, but are not healed enough to help me crawl out of here, and even if I could crawl out, I don't think I could use them to scramble up the walls of the rock to escape into the forest.

Not that there's anything in the forest to escape into if that opossum is to be believed.

Noise pounds from above—the human. I pull myself in tight under the rock ledge, but can't stop my jowls from slavering at the thought of food. Yesterday, there was some meat that broke into thin strips over my teeth. I can't get too excited. The human needs to know that I am dangerous and will attack if he tries anything more than giving me food and water and going away.

Today he's brought some crumbly brown meat that smells just wonderful, and then I get a bite in my mouth and, scratch my fur, it's rich and delicious and dripping with fat. I can barely control my jaws, I'm so hungry and the meat is so good. I almost nip the human's long, nubby fore-toes.

He jumps his paw back, toes clenching into a ball.

Oh no. I stop eating. "I'm sorry, human," I whimper.

His eyes are wide. His face open. He doesn't move to attack. I lower my eyes, lick the stone. I hope he understands I didn't mean it.

He stands. But then he returns and leaves me the little pool of water. I take that to mean he isn't angry with me.

The human leaves. I hear him stomping around above me, something dragging along the ground, bumping on rocks, and then he's gone. The forest sounds echo in my gully—but not life, just bugs or a bird passing over. The sun crawls its way across the blue, and soon the shadows grow long, covering my rocky hollow.

I doze a little, though sleep isn't very different from being awake at the moment. Next time I glance up, moonlight glints between the cliffs. Cold air creeps down into my crevice and I shiver. I tuck my legs even tighter into my body, curl my tail over my throbbing paws.

"Ho, my, doggie! That human sure must like you to leave you such delicious grub."

I crack open my eyes to see the opossum again—ugh. "I told you I am not a dog."

"Well, you're close enough to a dog for the humans, I guess." The opossum sniffs around, finds a morsel I missed, and slips it into his jaws. "So, not-dog, what are you doing in this cave? Seems awfully tight in there."

I decide to just be straight with him. "I'm hurt. I don't know why, but the human comes here every day and brings me food."

"*Every day?* Wow! Definitely more dog than not." The opossum's so excited, his fur starts bristling and glinting with moonlight. "Plus now I know where I can stop for a snack when the scavenging's slow."

Oh no. I should not have told him about the human. "I told you, I'm not a dog. I'm a coyote. And coyotes are known to eat opossums."

The opossum looks me over, raises an eyebrow. "I'm going to guess then that there's a reason you haven't eaten me, and that it's not because I stink." I freeze because I did not expect any pushback from this prey. He sniffs me, purses his lips. "Oh yeah," he squeaks. "You don't smell great. Burned fur and . . . ugh, how long have you been stuck in there?"

I give up. It's not like the opossum can injure me more than I already am. I tell him my story, explain how I got stuck here. "How did you escape the fire?" I ask him.

He finds another of my meat morsels and shoves it into his mouth. "I didn't," he says, mouth full. "My kind aren't den builders. We follow the food, moving from place to place. I fell off my mother farther up the lakeshore, near a lot of human garbage but also a lot of humans. I've been following the lakeshore ever since."

"Wait, you fell off your mother?"

"Yeah," he says, relaxing into a story. "I crawled out of my mother's pouch along with twelve other hungry babies. We all hung on to her fur as she hunted, sometimes heading back into the pouch if we were hungry. I was close enough to her head to get a name—it's Teeth, by the way."

"Teeth?" It was a prominent feature of his, but I'm not sure that's the nicest thing to name someone for.

"Yeah," he says, continuing, "Mom named us for the first thing she noticed about us when she turned her head. There was Big Eyes, Claws, Itchy, Pink Nose, Tufts, Stink Butt, and me —Teeth—then the rest were too far back to get a name."

Stink Butt? I am so glad I was not born an opossum.

"Anyhoo, as Mom walked, sometimes one of us would fall off, and she didn't stop for stragglers. First went Nameless #4, then Itchy scratched herself right over the edge, then I got a little too excited about being in a tree with actual fruit, and Mom waddled off before I could climb back on. Been on my own ever since."

He begins sniffing around for more nuggets of meat. I cannot believe that he's so calm about this story. His mother just left him behind? And suddenly I feel terrible because isn't that what I did to my pack?

"Your scent just changed," Teeth says, pausing mid-chew. "Don't feel bad for me. I like living on my own. Move on as the wind blows, eat when I want, garbage as far as the opossum can waddle. Life is good." He leans back on his long, hairless tail.

"Coyotes aren't like that," I whuffle. "I had a pack."

"Where are they?"

"Somewhere else, or the fire . . ." I manage to yip.

"What about the fire?" Teeth asks like it's not obvious.

"They haven't barked or howled since," I try to explain. "They haven't answered my calls. They haven't come for me."

Teeth waves his tail. "That means nothing. I passed plenty of animals who ran from this fire as I came down the lakeshore. Most of them assumed anyone left behind was a goner. Heck, that's why I came! I'm a scavenger and there are things here to scavenge."

"Ugh, gross."

"Don't tell me you haven't eaten the odd carcass."

"No, but I just would never . . . put it that way."

Teeth shrugs and begins preening his whiskers. "I like putting things straight." He slides a toe along one whisker to its end, then lets it spring and sparkle in the moonlight. "How about I make you a bit of a proposition."

"Proposition?" I yip.

"Yeah, a deal, a you-scratch-my-butt, I-scratch-yours situation."

"I don't want you scratching my butt—"

"It's a *saying*," he says like this conversation is so exhausting already. "Anyhoo, since you're stuck under that rock, how about I look for your pack for you?"

My ears prick up and my head lifts at the suggestion of such hope, and I bang my skull on the cave's roof. *Ouch!* I swallow the pain and woof, "You'd do that?"

"Sure," he says, waving his tail again. "Easy peasy."

"Why?" I'm so confused.

"Well, that's the you-scratch-my-butt part," he squeaks. "You say this human comes here every day and gives you food? How about you leave a little bit on the side for old Teeth here, and I'll use what daylight I would otherwise spend scavenging looking for your pack?"

He continues to groom himself while I chew the *proposition* over. The human doesn't bring me much in the way of food to begin with, and now I'd have to share it with this opossum? Then again, what's to stop this opossum from just coming and taking my food? I'm stuck and he knows it.

And even knowing that, he's offering to help me.

"I'll do it," I woof.

The opossum's ears flick forward. "You will? Oh, this is delicious!" He squeaks and cavorts in a circle. "Okay," he says, "great. So, when does the human come by here?"

"Mid-sun, or later."

"Perfect, perfect. So I'll scuttle off and start looking now, and I'll be back after the sun drops away with what news I find."

"And I'll save some food from the human for you."

His fur is practically vibrating with excitement. "Deal," he says, holding a paw out.

I lick his toes. "Deal."

As he clambers out of the crevice, I allow myself to believe that he'll find my family. I indulge in the hope that this is going to work, and that this isn't the craziest thing any coyote has ever agreed to.

sixteen

Gabe

IT'S NOT HARD TO SNEAK out of the lunchroom. I've been doing it every day this week and no one's noticed. My new lunch spot? Café Under-the-Stairwell. I just make lunch at home before going to bed, then grab it, a granola bar, and my water bottle before anyone wakes up and ride my bike to school. Then I hang out on the back stairwell until they open the doors and —*boom*—I can make it through to dinner without having to talk to another human being.

Except Zach, but he doesn't really talk. Monday, we began hauling out the dead wood blocking trails or where he wanted to spray vermicast, which I learned is worm poop—gross. By Wednesday, we had it cleared. Yesterday, we started spreading the worm poop and putting these hay rolls around. The idea is that the hay rolls will stop the soil from washing away as the worm poop helps the invisible good stuff grow back in the soil. I asked him when we would start planting stuff. He kind of laughed and was like, *Dude, the trees are going to have to replant themselves.* Then he rubbed his fingers together, meaning planting stuff cost mad money.

It was the first time I thought about the fact that what we were doing cost money. I mean, not my labor obviously—*thank you, community justice center!*—and maybe this is just a regular part of Zach's job, but those hay rolls looked expensive, and Zach said he rented a backhoe to clear some of the bigger brush without me. I kind of thought that this was, like, what the government does, right? They fix the broken stuff that everyone uses. But our town had this huge budget battle last year over school funding. I remember my parents sitting in on angry internet meetings with other people from the town, complaining about taxes and worrying about the cost of a new building. If the town can't afford to replace the old heating system in an elementary school, they probably don't have it in the budget to pay for baby trees.

I actually looked up how much baby trees cost. It was a lot more than I thought. And when I did the math on one tree per ten square feet over the whole of the burned patch at Rockledge, it added up to major money.

It's stupid, I know, but I had this idea. My parents kind of let our backyard go this summer—I get it, both my parents were out looking for work. But the upshot is there are all these baby tree sprouts in our garden plots. I bought some plastic cups on my last recycling run, and tomorrow I'm going to dig up all those seedlings and sneak them into Rockledge. I mean, I can only plant like ten or maybe even twenty baby maple and oak trees. That'll cover one tiny patch of the dead area.

But I'm still going to do it.

Today's lunch project, however, does not concern trees, but my dog — er, coyote. The local news station did a story on "Victims of the Fire" — it's been a slow news week, I guess — and the park ranger guy assured some worried callers that the hunt for the rogue coyote had not been called off, but that they only had so many rangers and were spread a little thin. So she's not safe. Right now, I'm researching if there's some community justice center for wildlife, a place where maybe she could be rehabilitated or something and then released. Or if there's some appeal process within the Fish and Wildlife Department, where I could plead her case . . .

"Mr. Meyer, I keep finding you here," a familiar voice states.

"I was just leaving," I say, shoving my phone and the remains of my lunch into my backpack.

Mrs. Dooley folds her arms — she doesn't buy it but doesn't seem that upset. "It's rather an unhygienic place to eat, under the stairwell."

I shoulder my pack and scurry up the stairs away from her. I don't want to give her attitude—I'm sure that wouldn't go over well at the justice center—but also is she dense? I mean, I'm not going to sit alone at a random table in the cafeteria and pretend that everyone in the room is not whispering about me.

"The cafeteria is out that door." Mrs. Dooley's voice booms up at me through the stairwell.

The sun blazes through the window in the stairwell, making the whole place feel like a furnace. There's still ten minutes left in lunch. Might as well go outside.

I sneak out through the cafeteria doors and am immediately in the middle of a basketball game. Cora and her gang are gossiping in the corner; they glance over at me, then huddle back up. Ophelia mouths the word *FREAK*. I want to pull out my phone, catch all this on video as proof for the next time Mrs. Dooley asks why I'm under the stairs, but instead I just turtle my head between my shoulders and plow across the pavement toward the woods.

"Yo, it's Mey-ro the Pyro," a voice shouts. "Caught your video last night. What's it like, being in a cop car?"

"Yeah," another chimes in, "what's the inside of a jail cell look like? Is it like on TV? Is the toilet just, like, sitting there, where everyone can see?"

"I was thinking of asking you to help me rob a bank, but then I was like, I don't want the guy who got caught on my crew."

Inside me, the pressure builds, like a soda can I keep shaking and shaking and shaking. I'm three-two-one primed to explode . . . but I hold it in, push it back, keep stomping across the pavement, definitely not running because running would make this so much worse . . . I will not blow. I am not ruining everything because of these jerks.

"Did they put you in handcuffs?"

"In movies they pat you down—did the cops pat you down? Like spread-eagle on the cruiser?"

All different voices now, but I am not looking up. The earthquake presses against the backs of my eyes, the inside of my brain. I am almost to the grass.

"What's it like being locked down in the slammer?"

"Meyer loved it, being locked up with the rest of the losers!"

That voice stands out: Taylor. My fingers curl into fists and it feels good, like this is what all that pressure inside was building toward, like this is the release I need. I turn on my heel, am angled perfectly to slam Taylor in his perfect face.

"Shut up, Mahoney." It's Owen's voice.

"Why are you getting involved?" Taylor snaps.

"Just leave him alone, man." He's standing on the sideline of the soccer field. The game is still going on behind him.

The shock of the interruption breaks the pressure inside my arms, my head, and I remember that I was walking away, that

I *have* to walk away from this kind of thing or I will ruin my whole community justice deal.

I hit the grass, keep going, and make it to the trees without hearing another thing. I cannot believe Taylor started with me. I am absolutely going to rat him out.

But if I say anything now, everyone will think I'm making it up because he made fun of me, to get back at him.

That's why he started with me, isn't it? Insurance. I can't tell on him now, even if I wanted to. I can't tell on any of them.

The scream builds inside, and I start kicking the leaves, the tree trunks, whatever is in my way until I slip and collapse onto a stump. I'm sweating. I dig my fingers into the wood and just focus on slowing down my heart, because it is slamming into my chest and I can't breathe.

I was never like this before, or it never felt like this before. Fine, I was mad, at my parents, at Liz, at Owen and Leo, at basically everyone. But it never felt this out of control inside.

The bell rings. Everyone else starts running for the doors. Except Owen. He's peering across the field. Is he looking for something? For me?

Nice that he's so interested in my well-being now, when he can't be arrested along with me. Where was that kind of interest two weeks ago?

A teacher waves for Owen from the door, and he goes inside.

For some reason that makes me sad. Why did Owen stick up for me? It would have been easier if he hadn't.

I haul my body up off the stump and begin loping toward the school. I force my feet to run, but my chest feels like a sponge that it is just sucking up all the sad in the world and it is so heavy.

I push into the door just as the second bell rings.

"Running late, Mr. Meyer?" the lunch monitor says as I drag my way across the cafeteria.

I don't bother saying anything back. I make it to the science room and grab the bathroom pass.

The basement bathroom is empty as usual. I hide in the last stall, the dark one in the corner, and sit. The door in front of me is dented from where I punched it. I pull out my phone, call the number Ms. Andrews gave me.

"Hello," she says. "East Burlington Community Justice Center."

"What if I am angry?" I say.

"Who is this?" she asks, then adds, "Gabe?"

"Yeah," I say. "I think you were right. I feel . . . angry."

"Oh, well, okay." There's muffled shuffling. "We talked about this, right? It's not the feeling that's the problem. Feeling angry is normal. It's what you choose to do with the anger. Are you in trouble, Gabe?"

"No," I say. "I was just feeling . . . angry."

"And what did you do about it?"

"Nothing."

"Well, maybe that's part of the problem. Feelings, especially big feelings like anger, can't just be bottled up; you need to do something with them. The trick is making the right choice about what to do with your anger. For example, if someone's bullying you, and it makes you angry, you could choose to hurt the bully, or you could choose to take a different action. You could talk to the school counselor or a teacher. You could talk to your friends about it. You could confront the bully.

"Whatever you do, it's not good to just bottle up the anger inside. Anger wants to be turned into action. You just need to think about what action to take."

"Yeah," I say, "Thanks. Okay, bye."

I hang up. This lady hasn't been to middle school. Talking to a teacher isn't going to do anything. And I'm not talking to my so-called friends at the moment. And me . . . confront Taylor? Last time that happened, I burned down a park.

But there are other actions. Riding my bike is one—I don't feel angry when I'm riding. There's my coyote, helping her. There's digging up the baby trees in my yard, the thought of planting them in secret.

It's weird, but thinking about that stuff makes me feel a

little better. I flush the toilet, just for show, and head back to class.

~

This past weekend, it rained Saturday, so I didn't get to plant my trees until Sunday. And then I also had to collect cans, which didn't go well. I wonder if maybe I've collected all the cans? There were only like five and I looked everywhere. My grand plan for how to make money does not seem all that grand. School just ended, so I'm riding over to the park now, have a garbage bag all ready for any stranded cans, but there's nothing. I park my bike at the entrance and find Zach by our stump.

"I think we have a tree fairy," Zach says as I tie on my boots. "Someone's planting baby maple trees on the bare patches."

"Really?" I ask, pretending I have no idea what he's talking about, but really sweating because, oh man, what if I did it wrong?

"I mean, it's nice and all," he continues, "but the forest will also do its own replanting. These trees won't let that good soil we're establishing go to waste."

"So it will regrow itself?" I finish with the boots and slip on my gloves.

"It'll take time, more time than if we had a budget for plantings. You and I will have to watch out for invasives — non-native plants can mess with our soil and upset the system — but yeah. Ten years from now, it'll be trees everywhere." He shoulders his pack and starts walking. "Now the picnic area? The trails? They're what's not coming back without money and human hours."

The picnic area? That was down by the lake. That burned?

Zach waves a hand in my face. "Let's move, we've got road repair from the tire tracks to get started on."

I spend the next hour shoveling gravel into deep ruts in the road. I guess this dirt track was never meant for fire trucks. I bet Zach's going to have me help fix the trails next. But the picnic area . . . I remember it having a little pavilion with a picnic table. Who's going to pay for the beams to replace that? If Zach's any expert on the issue, the town's not pitching in for it. So no picnic area anymore.

I ate lunch with my mom there when I was little. It was a nice break from the rough sand on the beach.

Zach finishes smashing a cliff of dirt down with a hoe. The sun has begun to drop. He looks at his watch and is like, "Hey, you're good, you know."

I check my phone. I've been here for almost two hours. "Lemme just finish this hole." It feels weird to leave a hole half-filled.

When I'm done, I wave to Zach, who's packing away the tools. I act like I'm heading out of the park on a trail, but then double back once I'm out of his line of sight. I have to feed my girl.

When I slip down into the crevice, she hardly growls. I've brought her chicken—there was a sale this week on chicken thighs. I threw them in the oven after everyone went to sleep Sunday. I have enough to give her two whole thighs a day!

I pull out the Tupperware and her ears twitch, then her nose wiggles. Holy hemlock, and she's kind of rolling and scrabbling toward me. Can she get out of her tiny cave?

Oh my gosh, oh my gosh, oh my gosh . . .

I scramble back. She growls, then yips. She stops moving. Rolls back on her side.

I guess she can't get out.

That's a lucky break. I mean, not that she's still hurt, but just, I don't want to be attacked by a coyote. I have to remember that she's not my dog. I may be responsible for her, but it's different.

She starts whining. Okay, she's kind of my dog.

No, she's just my coyote.

But if she's started moving, what if she gets out? What if she wanders off and gets caught by the game wardens? They'll kill her, that's what. Anger boils my guts, burns like acid.

The coyote growls. Can she smell anger or something? I have to calm down.

I fill the water dish, drop two cooked chicken thighs in front of her snout, and climb out. What am I going to do about her, though? As I walk out of the park, I dig through my brain for an answer, but nothing turns up.

At the road, unchaining my bike, I hear banging. I need a distraction, so I ride my bike toward the sound and find a guy. He has gray hair and wrinkly skin, and he's wearing old jeans and a flannel shirt. He's hammering a wooden frame. In a corner of his yard, there's a pile of blackened wood.

"What are you making?" I ask, not getting off my bike.

The guy looks over, pauses in his hammering. "Chicken coop," he says. "Sparks hit my other one. Went up like a Christmas tree in summer."

"Oh," I say. I hadn't even thought about sparks flying from the fire. Wait, didn't the news story say something about a chicken coop?

"Saved two of my three chickens," he goes on, pointing to the porch where two red-brown hens strut. "That's Sunshine and Silhouette. Now they're waiting for a home." He begins hammering again. "I saw you, at the community justice center. I was at your meeting."

My blood freezes, and I'm also sweating. "Oh?"

"Yeah," he says, slamming the wood over and over.

"I don't remember anyone mentioning a chicken coop." I don't want to give up the fact that I saw the news, that I know anything more than was said at the meeting.

He shrugs, continues hammering. "You looked pretty freaked out. And I can make a new one."

"Can I help?" The words are out of my mouth before I can even think about them.

The guy looks at me, considers the offer. "You could drag over those sheets of plywood."

I hesitate because I don't even know this guy. His house doesn't look that great. The paint's peeling and there's an old car rusting under a tent thing, which I guess is his garage. There are weeds everywhere. All this makes me feel worse. This guy probably needs those chickens for food. And I burned his coop and killed one of his birds.

I drop my bike in the grass alongside the road and push through the gate in his fence. I lift a sheet of plywood. Man, these are heavy. I don't want to just drag it across the lawn and kill all the grass, so I heft the whole thing onto my back and haul it over.

"Where should I put it?"

The guy looks up, lifts his eyebrows. "Against the fence there," he says, pointing with his hammer.

I move the whole pile for him.

As I lay the last board against the fence, I realize it's full night. The one streetlight down the road is all the light I'm going to have for several blocks. "I have to go," I say.

The guy nods. "Thanks for your help." He lifts a board, takes a nail from his tool belt, lines it up with the frame.

I get on my bike, put a foot on a pedal. "I could come back tomorrow," I say.

He smiles, doesn't look at me. "You don't have to, kid."

"I know," I say, spinning the pedals backwards. "Could I come back tomorrow?" I don't know why, but it feels really important that he say yes.

He slams the nail in with one swing of the hammer. "I'll be here," he says. Then pulls out another nail, whacks it in in one stroke.

I take that as a *yes*, and push off and pedal through the night.

When I get home, Mom is clearing everyone else's finished plates. "What happened to you?" she says. "I tracked your phone and saw you were still near the park. Do they have you working overtime?"

"I stopped to help a guy," I say, grabbing a clean plate and piling on the food. I'm suddenly starving.

"A guy?" Mom says. "Gabe, you're grounded. That means no hanging out, no—"

"It's not like that," I say, interrupting. I put my plate in the microwave. "As I was leaving, I passed this old guy in his yard. Sparks from the fire burned his chicken coop. I asked if I could help. He said yes."

Mom scrapes plates into the compost bucket. "You asked if you could help some random guy?"

I shrug. "So?"

"Nothing," Mom says, and continues scraping, but I see her steal a smile on the sly.

That smile rubs me the wrong way. I didn't do it for her. I did it because . . . I felt like I should. But I don't say anything to her.

~

By Friday, Zach and I have finished filling in the ruts in the road, and Mr. Larkin—the old guy told me his name was Paul Larkin—and I have finished putting together the chicken coop.

"Now, we staple on the coated wire and we're done," Mr. Larkin says, sitting back on his heels.

He said *we*. Like I'm a part of this coop. Like I belong.

"Where's the wire?" I ask. It's dark, but I can stick around to finish.

He lifts off his cap, wipes his forehead on his cuff. "In the shed. Be back in a sec."

I sit on a nearby stump to wait. It's been cool to have this stuff after school. I like working with Zach on the park. It's actually fun to dig and whack things with a mallet. And even when it's not fun, it's something to do instead of sitting at home.

"Nice coop," a voice says. It's a woman walking her dog.

"It's not mine," I say.

"It's still a nice coop," she says. "Do you make these often?"

What a weird question. "This is my first."

She smiles, nods. "You should make more. There are a lot of people around here with chickens. I'm sure they could use a nice coop like that." She walks on.

It only occurs to me after she's gone that the better response would have just been *Thanks*.

"Here's the wire," Mr. Larkin says, dragging over the roll of thick silver mesh. He begins stretching the wire sheet over the frame. "You want to try using the staple gun?"

"Uh, yeah," I say, hands already out.

He shows me how to hold it, how I need to keep my arms strong for the kickback, then he turns on the air compressor and gets in position to hold the wire. The first staple sends shivers over my body, and I'm smiling like a maniac because it's just cool to blast a staple into wood with a power tool. We finish the whole thing in like fifteen minutes.

"Nice," Mr. Larkin says, switching off the compressor.

My arms are shaking from the work, and I'm sweating like I ran a marathon, but I can't keep from smiling because I *made* that. Well, helped make that.

"I need a drink," Mr. Larkin says. "Cola?"

"Sure, thanks," I say, slumping onto my stump.

He returns with two cans and hands one to me. We pop the tabs and I drink almost the whole thing in one gulp.

"Slow down," Mr. Larkin says, chuckling. "You don't want to drown."

I stop to take a breath, still smiling myself. "That's good."

"Soda tastes better with sweat, in my opinion." Mr. Larkin takes a sip.

"Thank you," I say after another sip, "for letting me help with this."

He shakes his head. "Thank *you* for helping me with my coop. The other one I built with my wife. But she died a couple years back. I don't know that I could have built this without a partner. So it's good you came along."

The night is cool, and the soda is frosty, but I feel this warmth inside me and it spreads, golden and bright, all over my insides.

We drink our sodas, listening to the last of the summer crickets chirping. When my can's empty, I ask, "Can I keep this?"

Mr. Larkin looks confused.

"I'm collecting recycling to earn money to pay my restitution," I explain. "I think I'm still going to be short, though. There's not a lot around now, after I collected last week, and there are other people who I think collect cans for a living."

"Problems need solutions," he says. He takes his last sip, then holds his can out to me. "Take mine, too."

"Thanks," I say.

As I look over our coop, I think about what that lady asked, whether I had made this coop. It was like she wanted the coop herself. *Problems need solutions . . .*

"This lady," I say, "she walked by and said a lot of people around here have chickens. That they might need a coop. Do you think that's true?"

Mr. Larkin shrugs. "People around here do have chickens."

"Do you think if I made a coop, one of them might buy it?"

Mr. Larkin thinks for a moment, then tips his head. "Could be."

Could be is not a *yes*. Do I waste my time on a *could be?*

"If your question about the coops is whether you could earn the money you need making them, then my answer is a firm maybe," he says, standing.

Maybe is better than *could be* . . . right? This little spark of excitement fizzes up.

"And if you're serious about it," he continues, "I'm happy to give you my leftover supplies. Probably enough to make half a coop or more."

The offer is more than I could have hoped for. "Uh, sure," I say. "Thanks—I mean, thank you."

"Least I can do to repay you for all your free labor."

"I owed you a coop."

He pats my shoulder. "So we both got something out of it. You better get home, now," he says, nodding at my bike. "Your parents will be worried."

I check my phone—yeah, it's late. "I can load some of the stuff into my backpack," I say. "Then maybe tomorrow, I can come with a wagon."

"How about I drop it by your house tomorrow morning?" he says.

"No, I mean, you're giving me the stuff, I can't—"

He holds a hand up. "It's no trouble. I have a truck, and I have errands to run tomorrow."

I open my mouth to protest, but he pulls out a pad of paper from his pocket and a little stub of pencil. "Just write the address, son."

I write it down. "Thank you," I manage.

"No trouble at all."

I pedal home slowly, winding down some side streets, but then my stomach growls and I have to hit a bathroom pretty bad, so I turn onto my street, into my driveway, leave my bike against the garage wall, and head inside.

I eat alone. Then lie in the dark of my room, listening to the world happen around me.

seventeen
Rill

THERE IT IS — the scritch-scratch of Teeth's humanlike paws clawing down my rock.

"Ho there, Scruffy!" he squeaks, sliding down in a shower of pebbles.

"Ho there, Teeth!" I yip. My fur trembles with excitement.

That's weird — why am I excited to have my food stolen by this opossum? And *Scruffy?* I told him my name was Rill . . .

Teeth appears out of the shadows, the moonlight hitting his silver-white fur. "What's for dinner?" he asks, rubbing his front paws together hungrily.

"Some kind of bird. Same as last night." My heart's pounding; under the rock, my tail thumps in a wag.

"And the night before, and the night before," Teeth says,

sniffing over his pile. "The human has to improve his variety. A coyote can't live on bird alone."

"You mean *you* can't live on bird alone," I yip.

He waves a paw at me. "What goes for the opossum, goes for the coyote." He sniffs the pile over, selects a choice bit of bone with meat dangling off, and begins gnawing away.

I pant at this. What an odd guy Teeth is, even for an opossum. But funny. Wait—could it be that I actually enjoy the company of this not-rodent?

No way. It's just that I've been stuck here with my own yips for too long. I've had no one else to talk with. That's it.

It dawns on me that I've never yipped with another animal besides a coyote.

"Teeth," I say, "how is it you understand me? No other animal I've met understands coyote."

Teeth swallows a gigantic mouthful, shrugs his little shoulders. "A guy like me gets around in a lot of different circles. I pick up a little coyote here, a little porcupine there."

"A guy like you?" I ask.

"A marsupial," he squeaks. "We pouch-babies are kind of on our own in the forest, and that leads to us having to reach across species lines more than others."

I've never spoken to anyone outside my family, not even another coyote pack. Could I learn marmot? No—it'd be weird to chat with a meal. But will I have to, now that I'm on my own?

"Do you miss them—your family, I mean?" I ask him to escape the sudden need I feel to hear Mother's bark.

Teeth shakes his head. "What's to miss? It was very crowded on my mom's back. Didn't smell so good." He picks over his pile again, selects his next nibble. "Anyhoo, as I said, opossums don't really get along with one another. My siblings were always fighting over every scrap of food. Mom seemed happy to be rid of every baby that fell off her.

"And I like being alone. I wander where I want to go. I eat when I'm hungry, not when some alpha tells me I'm allowed to eat. Speaking of eating . . ." He digs into the pile again, pulls out two fistfuls of meat, and shoves both into his pointy jaws.

His life is exactly what I wanted for myself. The freedom, the choices—no parent barking at you to put more effort into an attack, no burdensome pups sniffing around every meal you catch . . . But then I remember that shiver along my fur, waiting for him. Opossums are born to be alone, but are coyotes? No, we are not.

"Would you visit me if the human stopped bringing food?" I ask. The actual fear I have about this sneaks out in my yip: both my fear that the human will abandon me, but also Teeth, I realize.

Teeth swallows, then frowns. "If the human stopped bringing you food, you'd either be dead or you'd find a way out of that cave. So no, I would not come here to visit your corpse or an empty cave."

The opossum does not honey-over his squeaks. "Thanks, Teeth."

"What?" he asks. "It's the truth. You want me to lie to you? No, you don't. And the truth is, I also think this human is not helping you as much as you think."

"What are you squeaking about? You just said, if he wasn't bringing me food, I'd be dead."

"No," he says, cleaning a whisker. "That's only half of what I said. I said you'd *either* be dead *or* you would have found a way out of that cave. This human is making it so you don't have to choose between those two. And hey, I'm not complaining. It's nice to know I have a meal waiting for me even if the scavenging turns up nothing." He takes up another morsel, shoves it in his maw.

My fur bristles. "You think I'm choosing to stay stuck in this cave? That I want to be taking anything from a human? I hate humans. Human traps took my brothers."

"Look, there are humans and then there are *humans*, same as in any species," Teeth says, licking his claw. "Last time I saw a human, it screamed and began hitting me with some kind of bristled stick. Of course I froze, then blacked out—I wake up, she's still hitting me with the stick, and I pass out again. Let's just leave it that this was not my best day.

"You, on the other paw, have a decent human bringing you food and water."

"Maybe the human will stop feeding me," I whuffle softly.

Teeth hears me anyway. "Nah. Humans are always tossing treats to dogs."

"I'm not a dog," I begin.

"You're close enough," Teeth says. "Listen, the human's been back here day after day. I sense a trend."

"The night of the fire?" I yip. "I ran from the flames and ended up at a human den. One of the human cubs—a real little one—startled me and I nipped. The cub screamed and the grown humans came after me.

"Humans may like dogs, but they don't like coyotes. They don't like me."

Teeth finishes eating his pile and begins grooming his whiskers, then his fur. I rest my head on my paws and watch, waiting for him to disagree with me.

"Sniff this," he says. "Maybe this human is different. I mean, he must know you're not a dog by now. Maybe he's a weird kind of human, the kind that like coyotes. Maybe he'd even like a marsupial like me.

"But even if he does like you, what happens when I find your family?"

"If—" I begin.

"When," Teeth squeaks. "When I find your family, are you going to find a way out of that cave, or are you going to make a pack with this human?"

"That's the most ridiculous thing you've ever squeaked."

"Ridiculous or not, that's what we are now," Teeth continues, finishing his groom. "A strange little pack of a burned coyote, a weirdo human who likes coyotes, and an opossum."

I pant lightly. "That certainly is a strange pack."

"And I don't even do packs," he says, smiling with his pointy mouthful of teeth.

I sigh, shift on my paws. They hurt less, but still hurt. Could I get out of this cave? Do I want to chance injuring my paws again if I try? Not yet, not yet . . .

"Hey, I'm not trying to make your tail droop," Teeth says. "I just think you should be thinking about this. If I come back tomorrow with news of your family, what will you choose?"

"What would you choose?" I say, avoiding his intent stare.

"I never had the choice," he says, sounding just the slightest bit growly. His mother waddled off without him, without even squeaking goodbye. How much of his professed love of lonely living is an act to cover those growls? And his kind are meant to live alone. What growls live inside Mother and Father, even the pups, for me, seeing as I did the same thing to them—just turned tail and ran?

"I'm not sure I have one, either," I yip. "I kind of abandoned my pack before the fire. Even if I want them, I'm not sure they want me back. Father called out for my younger siblings just as the fire started, but he didn't call for me." Strange how sad I feel admitting this to Teeth. Admitting it to myself, really.

"You're basing this off one howl?" Teeth asks, incredulous. "Could be you didn't hear him right. Anyhoo, families fight. I fought plenty with my siblings, and I've seen every other species go at it in my wanderings: raptors kicking fledglings out of the nest, skunks nipping at each other. The problem isn't that you fought; it's that you never got to finish the fight. You never got to the snuggling and licking part, where everyone makes up.

"Point is, it's never too late to try to patch things up if you really want to. Might be it doesn't work out. Might be you decide this strange pack of ours is your best option. But it doesn't mean you don't try—if you want to, that is."

I sniff my paw, nibble an itch. What if he's right? "I guess I'll let you know when you find them," I yip finally.

Teeth shrugs. "Okay, Scruffy." He scrambles up the wall a bit. "I'll see you tomorrow," he squeaks as he climbs over the edge.

"See you tomorrow, Teeth."

All night, and all the next morning, I chew over his squeaks. If—no, *when*—I get my family back, will I want them? Or will

EIGHTEEN
Gabe

A KNOCK ON MY DOOR wakes me Saturday morning.

"Gabe," my mother's voice says, "there's some man here with what looks like scrap wood for you?"

I push myself up, peek out my window down at the driveway. Mr. Larkin's parked his truck full of my coop supplies on the side nearest the back gate. My dad is standing, hands on hips, looking at Mr. Larkin like he's a space alien. I throw on clothes before he loses me my building materials.

Running out the front door, shirt half over my head, I yell, "It's okay, Dad."

They both look at me now like *I'm* a space alien.

"Gabe," Dad says, using his In-Charge voice, "this gentleman was just telling me how you've been working with him on fixing his chicken coop?" The tone of his voice suggests he believes this about as much as he believes in unicorns.

"He's just here to drop off some extra stuff."

"Gabe has been a real help," Mr. Larkin says. "And he's good with tools. He has it in his head to make another coop, try to make some money."

"Well, as you know, he has to pay back the store owner," Dad says, like he's running this jail . . . which I guess he is.

I lift the roll of extra chicken wire out of the back of the truck. "I'll just bring the stuff into the yard," I say to no one in particular.

"Chicken coop should make that twenty dollars, and then some," Mr. Larkin says.

"It's certainly nice of you to give him this stuff," Mom says, hugging her arms around her bathrobe in the morning chill. "You sure we can't pay you for the materials?"

Mr. Larkin shakes his head. "Gabe and I had an agreement. No charge."

"He's taking his commitment seriously," Dad adds, like anyone asked. "He's doing his hours, every day."

I arrive at the back of the truck to grab another load. Mr. Larkin helps me lift some two-by-fours out of the bed. He smiles and gives me a nod.

"I have no doubt," Mr. Larkin says to my dad.

Mr. Larkin lifts some plywood sheets out of the back, and my dad hustles over.

"Let me help with that," he says. "I'm sorry, I should have offered sooner."

It's weird, but I don't want my dad mixing with Mr. Larkin. My dad's always treated me like I was just another thing sucking his hard-earned money out of his pocket; now, I'm also the degenerate who cost him an interview. I don't want Mr. Larkin to see me the way my dad does. So I haul an extra armload, and the three of us get the rest of the stuff onto the patio in one trip.

We walk back around front to the driveway, and Dad holds his hand out to Mr. Larkin. "It was nice to meet you."

Mr. Larkin shakes his hand. "Gabe's a good kid." He then turns, holds his hand out to me. "Good luck."

I shake it. It's weird, but I don't think I've ever had a grownup hold out their hand for me to shake. It feels important. Serious. Mr. Larkin looks right at me as we shake, then he releases my hand, gets back in his truck, tips his head at my dad, and backs out into the road. Before he leaves, he smiles at me again.

Something about that smile, him driving away, the whole morning already—not even twenty minutes—fills me with this feeling like the only thing to do is melt right there on the dead patch in the lawn. Or cry.

I would rather melt.

Mom and Dad head in the front door. "Hey, Gabe," Dad says as he steps inside, "you want breakfast?"

"No."

He stays there, hanging out the door for a few seconds in silence, before slipping back inside.

Like I would eat with them? I heard what he said to Mr. Larkin, and what he didn't say, but totally put out there. That he has to cover for me. It's just like Mom with her apology at the panel—to my parents, I've dirtied the name Meyer, and they're desperate to prove it's only me who's bad.

My eyes start to water and I am just like, *Absolutely not, Eyes.* I stomp into the kitchen, grab a granola bar and my Tupperware with the last of the roasted chicken thighs, fill my water bottle, and head into the garage for my bike. I pedal hard, harder, so hard my legs start to burn, so fast the wind chafes my face, and then the tears are just part of the sweat on my skin, caused by the wind hitting my eyeballs.

The woods are dark. Wind rustles the changing leaves, and some loose ones—brown, yellow, reddish-green—flutter down, swirling in little eddies of air. My feet crunch through the underbrush. And then I reach the firebreak, the black burned earth. The dead place I made.

I go to step onto the burned dirt, on my way to the one living thing in this desert—my coyote—and stop just in time.

There's a tiny bit of green.

A tiny green thing growing. Not one of the trees I planted, some of which died pretty quickly, but a little plant that just popped up on its own.

I kneel down. Poke the leaf to make sure it's real.

It's happening. Just like Zach said.

It's coming back.

The tears still drip, but I also feel this lightness inside that becomes a smile, and then I'm laughing a little because it's coming back. All on its own.

I burned this place, but not forever.

~

My girl barely growled at me, and the sun has come out, so I am taking this plus my tiny green sprout as a good sign for today. Back home, I pull out my phone and search for chicken coop designs. Looking at all the materials, I realize that having built a chicken coop with Mr. Larkin is not the same thing as me building a chicken coop on my own.

There is a lot of math involved in making a chicken coop —area, angles, lengths, widths. I'm going to need paper.

I head inside and my dad is doing dishes. I make for the stairs. I have paper and pencils and maybe a ruler in my desk.

As I come back—I had a ruler!—Dad interrupts my train of thought.

"You starting to build?"

"Uh, yeah," I say, opening the back door.

"You need any help?" He dries a plate, puts it on a pile.

"No," I snap, not even thinking.

He flinches like I bit him, but what? He expects me to be all cool with him helping after this morning's little show?

"Okay," he says, diving his hands back into the sink. "Just let me know if you need anything."

I hesitate at the door for a second. That's weirdly nice-sounding for my dad. One time, I asked him to help me memorize this prayer for Hebrew school—he's the Jewish one, not Mom, and Liz was at one of her endless practices, so he was my only option. He snapped at me like I was totally out of line to interrupt him watching the news. I've never bothered to ask him for help since. But then I remember what Liz said, how I have to let people help me.

"I need some tools," I say, because, well, I do.

Dad drops the bowl he was scrubbing back into the sink, wipes his hands on a towel. "I think I have everything you might need."

"A staple gun?" Now we're talking.

Dad stops, looks like he smelled something gross. "Staple gun?"

"Yeah," I say, "for the chicken wire."

He shakes his head. "I don't want you using power tools." He heads down the steps toward the garage.

He could just say, *I don't have any cool power tools*. But whatever.

He returns with an open wooden box, like a rectangular bucket, and it's got a bunch of old tools in it. Dad holds it out to me, looking at the box like he's kind of surprised it exists. "This was my dad's," he says finally. "He worked as a contractor, did handyman stuff."

I never knew my grandfather—he died before I was born. "Are they still good?" I ask, picking out the hammer.

Dad's face scrunches like I'm a jerk for asking. "These tools were built to last. Not like the cheap stuff they make today."

I have to will my eyeballs not to roll. "Okay," I say, and wrap my hand around the handle.

Our hands touch, just along the sides, but it sends a little shock up my arm, because my dad hasn't touched me in a while. You don't notice things like that until you do, I guess.

He pulls his hand away, letting the full weight of the toolbox hit my arm, and it drops.

"Heavy, right?" he says, nodding like I should be impressed.

"I've got it," I say, and head outside.

Moment over.

It takes me a half-hour to plan my design and figure out my dimensions. I then spend twenty minutes sorting through what I have, then an hour of measuring, another hour of trying to find two somethings to use as sawhorses, and the sun begins to set as I'm about to start cutting. I head inside to turn the patio lights on, and when I come back out, there's Owen by the fence.

"What's all this?" he asks like it's any of his business.

"I'm building something," I say, and pick up my first two-by-four.

"I guessed that," he says. "What?"

I place it so the line I have to cut is just over the edge of the cinder block I found—these are my sawhorses: cinder blocks. "I'm making a chicken coop."

"Is this for the community service people?"

"No," I say. I begin sawing. The teeth on this thing must be dull because I am barely making a dent in this wood. I have to really work it back and forth, and—man!—my arm gets tired quickly.

"You want some help?" Owen is still standing there.

"No," I say. My arm is shaking. This can't be good.

"*Can* I help?" He hops over the fence like anyone asked. "I'm doing wood shop this semester. I've got saw skills."

A laugh escapes my lips before I can stop it. "Saw skills?" I ask, looking at him.

He's smiling. "For real." He holds out a hand for the saw.

I give it to him.

Owen turns out to be really good with a saw. He demonstrates some tips his teacher showed him, and then shows me how to use the file in my grandpa's toolbox to sharpen the tiny teeth on the blade. We make all the cuts I need to start the frame.

It's full dark when his phone buzzes. "I have to go home for dinner," he says.

"Oh," I say. "Yeah. I should probably put this away."

He holds the saw and file out to me. "See you on the bus?"

I shake my head, no.

"Okay," he says, hitching himself over the fence. "Well, maybe I'll see you at lunch."

"Yeah," I say, but know that I probably won't see him. Now that Mrs. Dooley is prowling the stairwell, I'm back to eating in the library.

"Later," he says, and walks away.

"Later," I whisper, watching him go.

~

Monday at the park, Zach and I are cutting and laying in new trails where the fire took the old ones. It's a ton of work— clearing the rocks, digging trenches for the thick slabs of wood to make the edges of the trails or to create steps on the steep inclines up a hill. At least we're working on the burned areas, so we don't have to clear brush.

Zach and I don't talk much while we work. I get a trench finished for my first step and Zach says, "Time's up."

I check my phone. It's nearly five. "I want to finish these steps," I say, wiping my forehead with the hem of my shirt.

"Trying to clock out your service hours early?" he asks, voice sly like he's catching me in some plot.

That gets under my skin because he knows I'm not doing that. "It'll just be another five minutes," I snap.

"I didn't mean that you were trying to get out of work, Gabe," he says, backpedaling. "You've just put in a lot of extra hours. One more week of this and you'll be nearing your forty required hours."

I jam the shovel in the dirt, rest on the handle for a second. "I just want to fix it," I say. "I want to finish the job."

Zach nods. "I get it." He picks up his pickaxe. "Stay as long as you like."

We work until my arms are jelly and the sun is sinking. I'm so tired when I leave, I nearly forget my girl. But I don't.

I slide down the gravel and land in the hole, and there's something down here—oh, gross! It's a rat! No, too big. Ugh, and maybe it's dead? It's just lying here, still. And it stinks like the gym bathrooms that time the sewer backed up.

I freak out for a second because if there's a dead rat in here, for sure my coyote has cleared out, maybe straight into a warden's trap, but then she growls, and relief sends sweat running down my skin.

She's still here, still safe . . . with a dead rodent.

Whoa, did my girl kill this? From inside a cave? She's a pro.

She growls at me again, just to show how not-tame she is, and I'm glad to see that because she is wild. Once she's better, I'm going to help her get free. Maybe I can sneak her out of the park, or chase her off . . . I'll figure it out. But what if she gets free on her own? I wouldn't know if she'd been caught, not until the news reported her being destroyed.

Panic sends spikes through my gut—no, I do not have the energy for this. I'll think of something. I have to think of something.

I leave her the meat I brought as an extra treat in addition to this giant rat-thing she killed. I fill the dish with the last of my water. Then I have to half crawl, half drag myself out of the crevice because I am so wiped out.

At home, Mom is actually waiting for me at the table.

"I was getting worried," she says, pushing a plate toward me.

"I stayed late to finish something," I say, taking the plate and the fork and turning to head up to my room.

"Gabe, come on," she says. "It's Rosh Hashanah, the New Year. I cut apples and everything."

I stop, look at the plate. Apple slices and a little bowl of honey sit beside the congealed meatloaf. The symbols of a sweet new year. A chance to start fresh.

"I just—I miss having you at dinner," she says.

"Not enough to wait for me before eating."

She sighs. "I'm sorry. You're coming home late. Dad was hungry."

"You have your job," I say, not facing her. "I have mine." I walk up the steps, close the door to my room, and sit at my desk. I don't know why I said that. I don't know why I couldn't just sit down and eat with her. Like old times.

But a part of me wants her to feel as lonely as I've felt.

To miss me so hard it hurts.

I turn the lights off and crawl into bed, not even changing, not bothering to get under the covers, and wait for sleep.

~

Wednesday it rains, and the ground's too soft to do much work. Zach cuts us off at 4:30 p.m. sharp. "Not much more we can get done until this rain stops."

It's like a joke that as I bike home, the rain slows to a drizzle and stops completely as I pull alongside the back fence. My half-finished coop frame sits under a tarp. There's still light in the sky, so I decide to put in an hour.

I get going, nailing the pieces Owen cut for me over the weekend, and then see from my downloaded plans that I need a level. What's a level? I google that and find out it's a little like a ruler with a bubble in a tiny tube of water that you use to make sure something is flat. There's nothing like that in Grandpa's tool bucket, so I wipe my hands on my jeans and head around to the front of the house and open the garage door.

The light is already on, and there's Dad reaching under his car, wearing an old flannel shirt and stained jeans.

"Oh, hey," he says, wiping his hands on a rag. "You're home early."

"Rain," I say, walking in.

"Can I help you find something?"

"I need a level." Nothing in this rusty closet . . .

I turn, and my dad's right in my face. "Here," he says, and holds out a ruler thing with the little bubble tube. "Need help holding anything?"

I'm about to say no, but then I remember that the plans say you have to move two pieces of wood at once while also holding the level, so I guess I have to say, "Sure."

I turn and he follows me into the backyard. I get the piece I need, pass it to him.

"How's this?" he asks, setting it against the frame.

"Yeah, that's good." I set the level on top of the plank. "Just a little higher on that side."

He shifts the plank. "Now?"

"Yeah," I say.

Dad holds the wood steady, and I set the piece. We work like that—level, hammer, level, hammer—and get the whole frame together. It even looks right. Like it's going to be a real thing.

"You know, if you need more wood, we could check the dump for some scrap," Dad says.

"They have free wood?"

He nods. "We could also hit the mall and box stores. They sometimes give away pallets."

"That's wood?"

"Yeah, those things forklifts move big piles of stuff with. The little wooden platforms? They're called pallets."

"Huh," I say, because it's weird talking to my dad.

"If you want, we could go tomorrow. The East Burlington station is open late on Thursdays."

I'd have to leave the park a little earlier than usual, maybe feed my girl before I start my service hours. "Yeah," I say. "That could work."

The back door opens. "Dinner," Mom says. When did she get home?

"Just a sec," Dad says. Then he turns to me. "Need help cleaning up?"

"Sure," I say.

Cleaning up is a lot faster with two people.

When we get inside, Liz is actually setting the table—doing a chore like a normal kid, like there's no standardized test or college application hanging over her. Mom is serving up barbecue chicken with biscuits and beans from Chicken Tony's Take-Out. My favorite.

"I picked it up on the way home," she says. "Your dad texted that you boys were working on something, so he wouldn't be able to put dinner on."

Wait, what? "Dad makes dinner now?"

"Every night," he says, drying his hands off. "Wash up or you'll taste more sawdust than meat."

I stumble over to the sink and wash my hands. They all sit and wait for me to start eating.

"Thanks," I say, sitting.

"So what are you building anyway?" Liz asks, serving herself beans.

"A chicken coop."

Liz looks at Dad. "We're getting chickens?"

"Not for us," I say. "I'm going to sell it. To raise money."

Mom exchanges a glance with Dad. "Well, that sounds like a great way to earn the restitution money."

She had to bring that up. "Yeah," I say, not feeling like explaining the real plan—the plan to help rebuild the park.

"I could help you sell it once you're finished," she says, cutting her chicken carefully with her knife. "Facebook Marketplace might be a good place to start, or Front Porch Forum?"

"I could ask my friends to tell their parents," Liz adds. "Everyone's looking into urban chickens lately."

What has happened to my family? Has there been a three-person brain transplant in the last few days?

"Uh, yeah. Sure," I finally manage to splutter out.

Mom nods. "Great." She smiles, eats her chicken.

"We can take photos as you build maybe, so people know it's locally crafted," Liz says. "That's like *the* thing with the urban chicken people."

"Okay," I say, still trying to process my family being helpful and nice and everything.

"I'm taking the last biscuit unless I hear an objection," Dad says.

"Objection!" I shout, and he smiles, and then I smile as he tosses the biscuit at me before I can think to not smile.

The conversation moves on to other things—something at Mom's job, Liz's new test prep regimen, Dad's home oil change for the car—and I just eat and listen, and it's almost like it used to be, before junior high, before everything started sliding into the pits. It's the best meal I've had in months.

nineteen
Rill

"NO HUMANS?" TEETH SQUEAKS from the ridge above my cave.

It was only the one time that the human actually visited at the same time as Teeth, but no matter how many days pass, Teeth will not let it go. "No humans," I yip.

I hear the rattle of pebbles as he slides down. "Well, that's too bad, because I've been working on my Terrifying Hiss Maneuver. Check this out." He turns his face from me, then whips it back, mouth open, tiny teeth shining in the moonlight, and breathes out, making this little *hiss* sound. His fur bristles and shimmers in the light. He looks like a very angry rodent.

"Terrifying," I say. This move would not deter a single coyote, but I don't have the heart to knock him down when he is so obviously impressed with himself.

"You bet your butt it's terrifying!" Teeth squeals, hunching back on his haunches and grooming his paws. "I sent a mouse shrieking into the grass with that one."

"Wow," I yip. "A mouse? Really?"

Teeth nods, not hearing the sarcasm in my yips. "I can't wait to test this out next time some animal tries to start something with me. I'll be all, *Not today, Fisher Cat!*"

He slides his long paws over his whiskers in what I've noticed is his sign that he's impressed with himself. He's a little vain about his whiskers, to be honest. I once told him he had some food on them, and he turned, embarrassed, and began a grooming session that took so long I fell asleep.

"It's some stick-shaped meat mash inside intestines," I yip, lifting my nose toward the food.

"What?" He sniffs the pile. "Humans eat this?" He takes a bite. "Oh, it's delicious, but still, humans eat intestines?"

"I guess they do."

"Never smelled this in my trash, but hey, you learn something every night." He digs into the food.

I'm not eating much myself. I'm not moving, not doing anything, and I'm not that hungry. Plus, my insides don't feel so good.

"Oh!" Teeth squeals when he's halfway through his dinner. "I get here and I see you and I forget to tell you the most important thing!"

My ears prick forward.

"I think I found your family!"

My claws dig into the stone. It hurts, but I can't help it.

"How do you know?" I whimper, afraid to even ask, because what if he's wrong?

"Well," he grumbles, mouth full and spitting crumbs of meat, "I guess I can't be entirely sure. An opossum isn't exactly welcome company in a coyote pack and, deal or no deal, I'm not turning into a coyote snack." He squeaks a laugh at his little joke.

I am in no mood for jokes. "Why would you tell me you found them when you don't actually know?" I growl, frustrated like I haven't felt in so long.

"Smooth your fur, Scruffy!" Teeth squeals, shuffling back, away from my cave. "I'm not completely certain, but I heard them yipping and one of the pups was named Fern. You said one of your brothers is Fern, right?"

Fern. Yes, that's them. It has to be.

Another pack could have a pup named Fern in it. It's a common plant, probably a common name. But I never smelled another pack in this territory. And how far could an opossum waddle?

"Where?" I growl.

"Where?" Teeth says, sneaking back close to grab more food. "Where, where . . ."

He makes like he's having trouble remembering, I think so he can stuff more food into his face before I growl at him again. Teeth is my only connection to the rest of the forest, my only connection to anything. I don't want to scare him away. But sometimes, I just feel it inside. This growl that if I let it out, it will burst from my jowls and howl forever. Maybe I didn't always have it, maybe before all the trying to teach the pups to work as a pack, before I learned that no matter who catches the marmot, everyone gets to eat, even if it means the hunter goes hungry. Before I learned that no matter what I did, my parents would always blame me for what happened to my brothers.

Or that *I* would always blame myself for what happened to them. For leaving them in those traps and saving myself. For running in fear when I should have stayed.

It takes me several long, deep breaths to calm my fur. Teeth has munched his way through most of the pile.

"I'm sorry, Teeth," I whimper. "I didn't mean to growl."

Teeth eyes me over his shoulder, shoving a big chunk into his mouth. "Oh, you meant to growl. And I get it. You've been stuck there how long? A big active mammal like you, this is terrible. And I can only imagine the stink."

I hadn't even thought about the stink. Gosh, is my nose broken? Or is it just that my head's out here and the stink is . . .

"I don't want to talk about it," I yip.

"Well, it doesn't matter. I shall go back to the weird empty field where the humans keep their big, loud, smoky pulling machines and sniff out the names of the other members of the pack."

"Thank you, Teeth." Something about this conversation has opened a spring inside me and water is splashing out and I feel like I'm drowning, like no matter how hard I paddle my paws, I am sinking under the water . . .

"Hey, keep your nose up, Scruffy." Teeth dares to step close to my snout, to run his tiny paw over mine. "I'm going to find your family. And you are going to get out of this cave and rejoin your pack."

I don't have the strength to answer him.

He pats my fur, then waddles off into the shadows. Pebbles trickle down, meaning he's climbed out.

This feeling inside is so strong, I can't move or even sleep. Moonlight shadows crawl along. Night noises—creaks and cracks, crunches and snaps; the echoing call of an owl—fill my ears, but I am drowning inside in silence . . .

~

The sun rises. I am left exhausted from my sleepless night with one nugget of a thought stuck in my jowls: That I'm ashamed of how angry I was at the pups and my parents. That instead of helping my pack, I turned tail and followed my own track. That

I thought having a family to care for was some rotten thing I had to drag along rather than the strength of having many jaws and paws around to help when you need it.

I chew that nugget as the sun passes over me. I really get my teeth into it and roll it around my tongue. Because I want to remember it the next time I see my siblings — and there will be a next time, there *has* to be a next time — and want to bury them in the mud.

I want to keep close to my nose that a pack can be frustrating, they can make you want to leave them forever, but they also are the warm body beside you in the den on a cold night, they are the other set of jaws defending your territory, they are a part of your world, and you are a part of theirs.

That maybe the world isn't half as nice a place without their annoying fur rubbing in your nose in the morning and curling up beside you at night.

For them, I try to move. I place my paws down and test the stone against my claws. It hurts, but not as much as before. My head whirls like a leaf in a stream, but I force my paws to pull me forward. My legs ache, my back aches, every part of me aches — how long have I been stuck here?

I move less than a paw's length out of my hole.

But it's something. The first move in the long trail out of the darkness and back to my family.

TWENTY
Gabe

"NO, DAD, OVER HERE," I say, pointing to where the end of the chicken wire should connect.

"Right, right," he says, stretching it the opposite way over the frame.

We've made three trips to the transfer station and one trip around the mall to the box stores and collected a ton of free stuff: nails, wood, wire, shingles, and more! So when we finished the first coop, it seemed silly not to make another. Then Liz snagged some leftover paint from the high school's theater department and gave the first coop a makeover. She's certain that "urban chicken enthusiasts" want funky painted coops. Mom helped me make a really cool ad on Facebook Marketplace and some other sites, and I guess Liz is right—we've gotten two emails inquiring about the coop, even though I put the price down as fifty bucks! With that kind of money coming in, I can pay my restitution and have extra to give to Zach for trees and materials.

I hammer the last staple down over the wire and we sit back, wiping sweat from our faces. It's a hot day for October.

"You want something from inside?" Dad asks, pushing himself off the patio. "I need a drink."

"Sure," I say.

I think we might even have enough for a third coop, if we don't waste anything. If I sold that one, just think: I could buy more wire, maybe better hinges than the ones we pulled out of a set of cabinets someone was just throwing out last weekend . . .

Dad hands me a glass of water and tells me he has to head out to do the food shopping.

It's Sunday evening, and my parents, Liz, and I have managed to finish two coops, paint and all. All I have left to do is touch up the trim on the second. Liz is studying, and Mom had a work thing she had to finish, so I have the whole yard to myself—a rare situation. Every day after community service, I've been doing something with one of them, either building, posting on websites—Mom made a Facebook page for my coop business!—scrounging supplies, or painting with Liz. It's like I've gone from never seeing my family to seeing no one but my family.

Oh, and Zach, I guess. We've nearly finished rebuilding the

trail through the burned part. And there are little green things everywhere—I bet the sun this afternoon will make it so that by tomorrow those little greens will have become, like, serious greens.

And Mr. Larkin. I ride by his place after community service nearly every weekday. He told me he had soda left over from a Costco run and needed my help finishing it, and it's nice to have a cold soda after digging dirt for two hours. He gave me a bunch of wildflower seeds he said his wife collected to spread over any bare patches in the park in the spring, but I wonder if there will be any bare patches.

"Yo, Meyer." Ugh, it's Leo.

"I'm busy," I say, sliding a paintbrush along the wood.

"Hey, yeah, no, that's why we're here."

I look over my shoulder, and there are Owen and Leo standing near my fence. "What do you mean, that's why you're here?"

"I've seen you and your family working out here," Owen says. "It's really cool that you are building these things together. I mean, they look sweet."

"What are they?" Leo asks.

"Chicken coops," I say, pointing to the little doors. "For backyard chickens."

"You guys getting chickens?" Leo asks.

"No, he's selling them to pay back . . . you know." Owen can't even say it.

"I'm selling them to pay my restitution for the fireworks and also to raise money to rebuild stuff in the park." It escapes my mouth before I can even think about it.

"Rebuild stuff?" Leo asks.

"That's awesome," Owen says before I can say anything. "Can we help?"

I think about it for a second—it was nice having some time to myself to just think, but maybe with those two, I could get a start on a third coop?

"I guess," I say. "But this is no joke," I add. "It's real work."

Owen hops over the fence. "I have saw skills, remember?"

"I learned how to use one of these in wood shop," Leo says, picking up the level. "Just tell me what to do."

"I guess maybe start measuring and cutting those boards for a new frame?" I say. I hand Leo the plans.

Owen smiles. "Cool."

"Nice," Leo says, looking over the design. "Did you draw this?"

A smile forces its way into a corner of my mouth, even though I gave my body strict orders to play it cool. "Yeah," I say, looking down at where I'm painting.

"This is awesome," Leo says.

"Allen," Owen sing-songs in response.

And then I can't help but smile full-out across my whole mouth.

"That's just the worst cheer," I say.

"It's junior high," Leo says. "Everything's supposed to be the worst."

"Have you smelled the locker room?" Owen says, pulling the measuring tape across a board. "The worst."

"Have you eaten the cafeteria food?" Leo says, drawing a line where Owen points. "The worst."

"Have you met the jerks on the field at recess?" Owen says. "The *worst*, including me."

"Including me, too," Leo says. "I'm sorry if I've been a jerk, man. I was freaking out."

"Yeah," Owen adds. "And Taylor, he's kind of been a major jerk."

"Major," agrees Leo, nodding.

Something settles inside me, just this tiny shift, like a piece of wood sliding into place, and it's not weird being with these guys. Or maybe I just don't feel as weird being with them.

I shrug their eyes off of me, look down at the line of trim. "I'm over it," I say.

"We should have stayed," Leo says.

"No," I say. "I shouldn't have stolen the fireworks, and I shouldn't have shot my firework at Taylor's feet." I'm about to say, I was just so angry about him, but I'm too embarrassed to admit what I did, or that I was so mad, I wanted to burn him and the forest just got in the way . . . "Anyway, it was my idea," I finish. "And I like the job fixing the park. It feels good to, like, do something to make up for what happened."

Leo nods. "I hear that."

"You want this in the pile with the other wood, or should we start a new pile?" Owen asks, holding up the freshly cut piece.

"New pile," I say, grateful to get away from talking about real stuff.

We work like that until the sky goes orange, just painting and cutting and measuring and chatting. Not about the fire, but stuff from school, what they're doing in soccer, what I've been doing with Zach. My dad calls from inside that dinner's ready, and the guys help me clean up everything and put it under the tarps on the patio. When they leave, it's kind of normal. We just say bye and see you at school and slap hands and it's just . . . normal.

"It might rain tomorrow," Owen says, jumping the fence.

"Yeah?" I say.

"So you might want to ride the bus," he says.

I shrug. "Maybe," I say.

"Don't maybe me," Owen says. "I want to see your butt on that bus. I'm sick of sharing a seat with this guy." He hooks a thumb at Leo. "The toast crumbs fly everywhere."

Leo shoves him in the shoulder. "The bus bounced on a pothole!" he shouts.

"Later," I say, and they wave as they walk back up the street to their houses.

Inside, I ask if I can set the table, and Liz says she'll clear, and Mom calls that she's almost done, and Dad hands me the plates and stuff, and there's this warm feeling inside my chest, like I'm home, like a real home. Like I'm happy.

~

I sell the first two coops Monday, giving me a cool hundred bucks for my park fund. I feel like I should tell Owen and Leo, and I see them in the hall before lunch on Tuesday, but they're talking to some other soccer kids, so I decide to wait. Mom told me to pay off my restitution ASAP, so I leave school right at the bell to squeeze the payoff in before my service hours.

Inside the justice center, Santa—I mean, Mr. Darling—is sitting at the front desk. "Gabe, right? Can I help you?"

"I'm here to see Ms. Andrews."

"I'll let her know."

I sit down in one of the chairs and pull the cashier's check out of my backpack. Twenty-three dollars and seventeen cents exactly.

The door opens, and Ms. Andrews appears. "Gabe, what a surprise!"

I stand, hold out the check. "I have my restitution, paid early and in full."

"Oh," she says, something hesitant in her voice. "Well, come on back to my office and I'll make a note."

I follow her down the hall to her office full of plants. I sit in the same chair as before. "So, here's the check," I say, holding it out again.

"How are things going?" she asks, taking the check and putting it in a zippered pouch.

"Do I get a receipt?" I ask because no way am I paying twice if she loses that check.

She raises her eyebrows. "I'll give you one," she says, and pulls out a pad. "Zach says you're doing great work at the park."

She's trying to get me to talk. Ugh. "Yeah, it's good, I guess."

"And how is everything else going?" She's writing out my receipt really slowly.

"Fine," I say. Do I really need the receipt?

"How's it going with the angry feelings?"

She has to bring this up? "It's fine," I say, a little snappish.

"You didn't sound fine when you called two weeks ago. How are things at school?"

I check my phone—if she keeps dragging this out, I'll be late to meet Zach. "These kids were just—look, seventh grade stinks."

She smiles. "I remember it well. But I hate to tell you, the kids who make seventh grade stink, they don't disappear in eighth or ninth grade."

"I've just got to ignore them."

"Sometimes," she says. "But sometimes ignoring a problem only makes you feel worse."

"I think I'd be breaking the contract if I hauled off on the guy who's bullying me."

"Is that the only option you have?"

I swivel in the chair. "It's the easiest."

"But *is* it that easy to hit someone? And what about after?"

I think about my hurt hand, imagine being dragged to the principal's office. "Okay, maybe it's not completely easy."

"So maybe see if there's someone at school you could talk to about it in the guidance office. Maybe brainstorm some other ideas for how to handle this bully."

I wonder if Mrs. Dooley counts as someone. "Maybe," I say, imagining her hauling off on Taylor for me.

Ms. Andrews rips off the receipt and holds it out. "Congratulations on paying the restitution."

I take it. "I earned it all myself. Collecting recycling, and then I built and sold a chicken coop."

"That's fantastic!"

"My family helped. My friends, too. Make the coop, I mean. That's okay, right?"

"It sounds like you have a great team behind you."

I hadn't thought of them that way. "Yeah," I say, smiling. "I guess. Okay, well, I have to get to my community service."

"Keep up the great work," she says.

I nod, shoulder my backpack, and wonder the whole bike ride to the park at the fact that I have a team now. In a month, I've gone from nothing and no one to a team.

~

Zach has me pulling buckthorn shoots—they're invasive in Vermont—so it's easy for me to sneak over to my girl. I slide down into the crevice, waiting for my growl. But there's no growl. I creep closer. Her head is slightly farther out from under the ledge, but her body is still wedged in the cave. She opens her eyes, watching me, but does nothing else. She seems different. Worse. I drop food by her nose. The nostrils twitch, but she doesn't move to lick it up.

Oh no.

My coyote is sick. Sick because of me, what I did, what I'm doing—she needs help, real help, not some stupid kid feeding her scraps. All the knots inside tighten, squeezing me, and suddenly I'm so angry—at her for being sick, at myself for not doing more, at everything—I want to tear myself apart.

I scramble out of the crevice. I need to scream, and I can't scream in front of my girl—I don't want to scare her. Standing aboveground, in the gray-black expanse of what I did, the anger fills every square foot. But I can't lose it, not now, not here. I'll figure something out when I get home.

I go back to pulling buckthorn. I rip up shoot after shoot,

and the anger's grip loosens with each bend in my hips. I pick buckthorn until my breathing slows to normal, and then more until I've got a full bag. I leave the shoots in Zach's truck for his compost pile and bike home crazy fast. Inside, I start searching around the Internet for dog medicine. There are a billion different kinds; I have no idea what she needs. And all the sites say I need a prescription from a vet. How am I supposed to get my girl to a vet?

I slam shut my netbook, the anger squeezing my muscles. I take a breath. Take another.

A knock at the door—Mom pops her head in. "Owen and Leo are outside."

My team. "I'll come down."

"Hey," Owen says. "We got out of drills practice early. We thought we could help with the next build."

"Actually, I could use your help with something else," I say, slumping onto the bench next to the picnic table.

"What's up?" Leo asks.

They look at me like they actually care. Like they're not just here because it's fun to saw wood.

"My dog is sick," I say. It feels good to even share just that.

"What dog?" Leo says, looking around the yard.

"Not dog, exactly," I say. I shuffle closer to them, and they lean in. Taking a deep breath, I tell them about my girl. "She's sick—well, I think she's sick. But I can't get her medicine without going to the vet. How do I get a coyote to the vet?"

"Wait, is this the coyote they've been looking for? The one that bit a kid?" Owen asks.

The anger strangles my words because who is he to judge her? But I breathe through it. "Maybe," I say, finally. "But she's good or, at least, I did this to her. She was scared by the fire, that's the only reason she bit the kid. And she got burned, because of me."

"Because of *us*," Owen says.

Leo nods. "We're with you on this, dude. We've got to save her. So what's the plan?"

I have to check their faces to be sure, but they are absolutely serious.

"Do you still have that wheelbarrow?" I ask Owen.

By the time Mom calls me in for dinner, we have it all worked out. Leo's family has this gentle muzzle thing that they use on their golden retriever sometimes, and his vet is on Shelburne Road. My girl looked pretty rough, so we agree that we can probably slip the muzzle thing on her, then load her into the wheelbarrow, cover her with a blanket, and wheel her to the vet's office. We have to wait until Saturday—Leo and Owen have practices and I have community service—but I think she can make it until then.

She has to.

TWenTy-one
Rill

THE CAVE IS COLD, OR I am cold—I'm not sure there's a difference between me and the cave at this point. All my efforts to prepare for Teeth's news of my family have gotten me a mere snout's length out of the cave's mouth. When the human came with my food and water, he did not even notice. Then again, he didn't linger or try to touch me this time. He's been rushing to get away from me for days now. In other circumstances, this would make me feel good—he's scared of me, he knows his place—but I am so lonely, his rushing away without even giving me a chance to growl leaves me feeling even colder than this cave.

Where is Teeth? The moon has been up for a while, and he's still not here?

It's just like him to forget me when I'm so very cold and in need of someone to yip with. I even left him most of the food. I'm not very hungry, and my insides feel rather jumbled and bad.

My body starts to shiver. It makes everything hurt worse.

The moon crosses over the crevice and disappears from my scrap of sky.

Where *is* Teeth?

He found out the coyotes he located are not my family and he's afraid to tell me, that's it. No, of course it isn't. Teeth would not give a hair off his tail to avoid telling me anything—he's just not that kind of rodent . . . or whatever he said he is. Martian? Soup pile?

So he's just late? No, never. He's been coming early these last few days, staying longer.

The sky seems to be getting lighter now. Could it be morning? No . . .

Yes. Definitely morning. And no Teeth anywhere.

What if he found my family in that strange field he mentioned, but when he tried to squeak with them, they attacked? Obviously not the pups, but Mother or Father. They might have seen him as a threat, even if he only hissed ridiculously with his mouth hanging open.

What if the pack was not my family? What if that pack attacked?

Oh, Teeth, I'm sorry.

I have to get to them, to him. Try to save him if I can.

I dig my claws into the rock and drag. The pain lightnings through my body—through my bones, my skin, shimmers out over my fur. But I dig harder and pull again.

I will save you, Teeth!

TWENTY-TWO
Gabe

"LIFT THAT SIDE!" ZACH YELLS from the other end of the log. "Higher! Yes!" We're installing some snake-rail fencing to mark the beginning of our new trail. One bad placement and the whole thing slides apart, so I lift slowly and then rest the top rail just so.

Zach slaps the top of the corner where the rails meet. "That's how it's done."

He pulls out his water bottle and I pull out mine. It's nearly empty—have to save some for my girl. Or is she *our* girl now?

I saw Owen and Leo at recess today and almost waved to them, but they were in the middle of soccer and I just didn't want to get into the wave and then have them not see it or maybe see it and not wave back. We may be a team in my backyard, but I'm not sure it extends to the schoolyard.

"We should get the post-hole digger from the truck for the sign," Zach says, wiping his mouth.

"But you just had me put it back in the truck," I say, fake whining. It's a thing we do now.

"It'll put hair on your back," Zach says in response, our other thing. Anything hard puts hair on your back, like this is a good thing.

I head down the dirt road—now complete with no ruts or potholes thanks to me and Zach—when there's a scream.

I turn and Zach's already looking around, into the woods, the burned area—the scream echoes.

Then the person screams again. "Get away!"

Zach is on his walkie-talkie, and we are both running toward the voice.

There's nothing in the way because the scream is coming from the burned area—our new path—and then we turn and I have this sinking feeling in my gut because we are running toward my girl, toward her cave. Did the person fall in? No, the path is nowhere near her cave. But maybe the person was off the path . . .

We clear a rise in the rock, pull up over a cliff, and it's worse than I feared: my coyote is in the middle of the path, lying on her side, panting.

TWENTY-THREE
Rill

MY BODY SCRAPES AGAINST THE rock. I pull harder. My claws scream. My paws throb.

The rock releases me slowly. I slide forward in bursts, then slide a little more with each pull. Finally, with one lurch forward, my rump escapes the rock, and I land on my side in the gravel at the bottom of the crevice.

I'm completely exhausted. But I am not even halfway there.

I begin to drag myself up the far opening of the crevice, where Teeth and the human have traveled.

Paw over paw, pull after pull, I move along the earth like a furred snake, too tired to lift my body out of the dirt. There is no stopping now, no resting. I have to keep moving or I might never move again.

The ground rises and I climb with it, up the gravelly dirt, and my nose tastes the fresh air of the forest.

I try to stand. My legs wobble. I fall over. I keep trying. I stand, take a step, fall.

A human appears. Will it help me? I stumble toward it. "Help," I manage to yip.

The human screams, scuttles back from me.

No, human, wait, I want to woof, but I have nothing left. My body falls away from me and I fall with it. The sun dissolves into sparkles.

TWENTY-FOUR
Gabe

THE SCREAMER STANDS over my girl whispering, "Oh my gosh, oh my gosh, it's dead," and then sees us and yells, "It just launched itself out of that hole over there and then came running toward me."

No, she did not, I think, but do not say. Something must have scared her out of her hole. That's my coyote on the path, burned paws and fur and all.

She looks worse out here, or maybe it's just because I can see where her fur was singed off. She's panting softly, barely breathing. *Please don't let her die,* I think.

"Where did this dog get so burned?" the person asks. "I mean, could it have been holed up somewhere since the fire?"

Zach shrugs, already on his cell phone. "Must have been," he says to her, then starts talking on his phone. "Yeah, I have an injured coyote here in Rockledge. Yeah, looks pretty bad. I'll text you the location, drop a pin on the map. Yep. Okay, great." He turns back to the hiker. "Animal control is on the way."

Wait—did Zach just call the animal cops?

"This is it, right?" the hiker says. "The coyote that bit that kid? Oh my gosh, it could have bit *me!*"

Panic starts in my gut, explodes through me, turning to anger.

She keeps yammering, "Do you think I should get a rabies shot or something? Just to be safe?"

Zach is somehow remaining cool. "If it didn't bite you, you're fine. We'll take care of it from here."

The hiker reluctantly backs away down the trail and continues with her walk. When she's far enough away, I jump on Zach, closing the space between us in an instant.

"You have to call them back," I say. "Tell them you were wrong. Tell them it's just a dog or something."

Zach puts up his hands. "Whoa, dude, personal space. What are you talking about? This coyote needs help."

"I'm taking her to the vet this weekend," I say. "Just call them back."

"Gabe," Zach says, putting a hand on my shoulder. "You must chill."

"There's no time to chill, Zach! Call them back!" I'm

screaming because I can't not scream because they will take her and kill her and it's all my fault.

Zach's voice changes. He stands taller. "Gabe, be straight with me. Did you have something to do with this animal?"

"Of course I have something to do with her," I yell—I can't do anything but yell. "She's burned, isn't she? I did that. But I've been helping her. I found her one day while I was working here. She was getting better, I swear. But the animal control people, they're going to put her down. They said it at my meeting and on the news. They think she bit some kid. But she was just scared by the fire. She's fine, she's a good coyote. She's good . . ." The word trails off because I start crying and can't stop. These big sobs like I'm a baby and I can't help it.

Zach kind of pushes me back until my knees hit something and I find myself sitting on a rock. "Let's take a deep breath." He bends down in front of me, both hands on my shoulders. "This animal needs medical attention. That's what animal control can provide. And it's a wild animal, so you cannot take it to a vet."

"But they'll kill her, Zach." I can barely form the words.

"Gabe, I need you to tell me exactly what you've been doing with this animal. It's important to give the rehabilitators who are going to try to save this coyote all the information we can."

"Please," I whisper. They're going to put her down, I know it.

"Gabe, focus," Zach says, cool-guy voice replaced by this all-business man. "Tell me what's been going on."

So I tell him because what if it helps the animal people decide to help her instead of turning her over to the game wardens? I tell him when I found her, how I've been feeding her and giving her water. That she's been good, never vicious. I tell him about the time she caught that big rat all on her own — try to explain that she's getting better. That I have a plan to fix her the way we've fixed everything else.

By the time I'm done, animal control has arrived. They have a long stick with a wire loop at the end and a crate. They realize pretty quickly that they don't need the stick, that she can't attack them even if she wanted to. They wrap her in a thick blanket and lift her into the crate and then she's gone. Taken from me.

Zach talks to the animal control people, tells them what happened, then tells them what I said.

The animal control person looks at me. "Gabe, is it?" she asks. "Hon, did you ever touch the coyote? Did she bite or scratch you?"

"No," I manage to say, tears still leaking down my cheeks. This woman must not know anything about animals because didn't she see my girl? She can't move, can't bite, couldn't scratch . . .

"Well, listen, Gabe," she continues, back on task, "I think it's important to get you a rabies shot, just in case. Coyotes are not rabies carriers, but this one's in rough-enough shape that we can't rule out an active infection. You've had close contact, so we need to make sure you're protected, okay? I can bring you to the hospital."

I nod.

"Can you give me a number to call your mom or dad?"

Zach steps up. "I'll give them a call and tell them to meet him at the hospital."

He holds out a hand for me, then, when I don't take it, he pulls me to my feet. "Gabe, let's focus right now on making sure you're okay."

I don't nod, don't do anything, because there's nothing to be done. My girl has already been tried and sentenced. And I can't help but feel like I've failed her.

I let the animal control lady lead me to her cruiser and drive me to the hospital.

~

I call Liz, but it's Mom who comes stalking into the emergency room, high heels clicking on the sanitized tile floor. "Oh my god, what happened?"

"Nothing," I say, sliding off the table. "I had to get a shot."

"Shot? For what?"

"Rabies."

"Oh my god, why!" She's practically shaking me.

And I have to explain to her about everything: finding my

girl, feeding my girl, and then finding her again, sprawled on the ground, half-dead, and I start crying again.

I swear I've never cried so much in my life as I have in this last month.

But it feels better. Not the crying itself, really—that's embarrassing. But as I finish talking and the tears kind of stop themselves with the words, I can breathe a little easier. Like every tear makes some space inside for air. Like I'm not choking so much down inside.

"Gabe, I—" Mom kind of swallows whatever she was going to say, then continues, "I'm so sorry."

I blow my nose, feel myself coming back to myself. "You didn't scare my coyote out of her cave."

"Your dad and I," she says, straightening her coat on her arm, then her purse, "we've had a hard year. And Liz is in this serious time in high school, when all of these huge choices have to be made. So there's been a lot. And I know you know that.

"But I also know we've done a bad job of keeping track of how hard this year has also been for you. And that's what I'm sorry about. I think we all thought, well, actually, I just don't think we thought at all about what was going on for you. So, just, I'm sorry."

"I heard you that night, after the fire," I say. "You said, 'Where did we go wrong?' Well, you didn't," I tell her. "I mean, what I did wasn't your fault."

"Oh, baby," Mom says, and now tears are dripping off her nose. "We didn't mean *you*—it's everything, the bills. We had just received a notice about an overdraft—oh, honey, I'm sorry you ever thought that. No, never you, Gabe. We—I am so proud of you."

She's straightened her coat so much while she's talked that it's completely off center and just slides off her arm to the floor. It lands in a pile with a *shlump*.

A laugh bursts out of my lips, and she smiles and laughs, and then I bend down and grab the coat and hand it to her.

"Thanks for coming to get me," I say.

She takes the coat. "I'll always come when you call, Gabe. No matter what, okay?"

I nod.

"And I'll always love you, no matter what." She takes my shoulders, looks into my eyes. "I do love you, Gabriel Joseph Meyer. No. Matter. What."

It's super embarrassing, having your mom stand there in the ER and stare into your face while holding your shoulders and say something like that, and I am squirming to get away with like 80 percent of my body, but 20 percent? It's totally there for that moment and I hear her words, and they are like water soaking down into dry dirt.

I lean into her hands, not sure what else to do, and she pulls me into a hug, and I let her, because sometimes, even if it's just

20 percent, you have to give in to the soft earth part of yourself. And it feels so good. Standing there in the middle of all those rushing people and beeping machines and big rolling hospital beds like rafts down the river of the hallway to just be held by my mom. To know that right now, even if it's just for now, it's me and her again.

She said she loves me, no matter what.

Right now, I can even let myself believe it.

TWENTY-FIVE
Rill

WHEN I OPEN MY EYES, there is no sun. There are tiny sparks of light, different colors, but not up in the sky. I sniff the air, and it smells of humans and unnatural vapors. I hear animal noises, and they all speak of fear.

Where am I?

I shift but am too weak to stand. My paws are wrapped in some thin skin, like a tough leaf. There's a clear vine running into my leg that leads outside this cave or whatever it is that I'm in. My head swims, but I feel no pain.

I close my eyes. I'm no longer in the forest, that is the one thing I know for sure. I am far from Teeth, from my family. I have no idea how to get back to them.

I am in no pain, but I have lost everything I loved.

I am alone.

A whine escapes my jowls, not even remotely a howl, but the sadness sometimes needs a voice. This feeble whimper does not begin to capture the lake of sadness inside me, but it is the start.

I may never stop howling.

TWENTY-SIX
Gabe

"I THINK WE CAN CHARGE more for these," Mom says from the kitchen where she's typing a response to the emails about our chicken coop post. Apparently, word has gotten out about cheap, local, handcrafted coops. We have four offers on the third one.

"It's the paint job," Liz says from her perch at the table.

"I think it's the good cause," Mom offers. We've added to the post that all profits are going to raise money for the restoration of the picnic area at Rockledge.

"I asked if you could look for news of my coyote," I remind her.

"I'm searching, I'm searching," Mom says, and opens a new window. "I'm not seeing anything," she says after several clicks.

"That's good news," says Dad. "If they were going to off her, there'd be a story."

The rumble starts in my gut and builds, revving from zero to full-rage race-car fast at the casual mention of my girl's impending death. The feeling is just there, completely beyond my control.

But there's the feeling and there's the reaction to the feeling. Dad doesn't mean anything bad. He's right, even. If they had put her down, they'd advertise the fact.

Deep breath in, deep breath out.

The earthquake quiets. The pressure inside deflates.

"I'll ask Zach this afternoon." Every day, I've harassed him. It's Friday now. There's got to be some news out of the rehabilitation facility. I've called, but they won't talk to me.

Mom shuts her laptop. "Time's flying." She gets up, slugs the last of her coffee. "I'm guessing you're riding your bike?"

I look out the window. It's gray, but not raining. "Maybe," I say. I grab the lunch Dad packed for me from the counter and head for the garage and my bike. But then I see Owen and Leo down the block heading for the bus.

I've been avoiding the bus for so long, I don't even remember the pickup time anymore. But there it is. Coming toward our stop.

I leave the bike. Run for the bus stop. Make it just as the bus pulls up.

"Hey," I say, breathless.

Owen smiles. "Finally." He holds up a hand to slap. I give him a weak slap back.

"Early morning carpentry?" Leo asks, climbing on behind me.

"Nah, just late."

"But you made it," Owen says.

We find seats near the middle—Owen and Leo on one, me across the aisle in the short seat.

"So what's the plan for tomorrow morning?" Owen asks. "I have the wheelbarrow and this old blanket ready to go."

I forgot to text them—we don't talk in school, and they've had practices every evening—and I wasn't 100 percent sure they'd remember. "The plan's off," I say. "The animal control people found her."

"What?!" Owen's face falls. "But that means—"

"I know," I snap, the anger bursting up. And it spreads, pushing from the inside, and I feel tears press the backs of my eyes.

"This is the worst," Leo says, resting his forehead on the seatback in front of him.

It's weird, but they both seem upset, too. Like they actually care. And somehow, them being upset makes the anger less painful. More sad.

No way I'm crying on the school bus. I turn away from them both and look out the window.

"We are not giving up," Owen says quietly.

"What?" I say. Leo looks over, forehead still pressed to the vinyl seatback.

"This coyote," Owen continues. "She was my chance to do something. My chance to make things right. I am not letting this go."

"Dude, she's in coyote jail," Leo says.

"So we figure a way to bust her out." Owen stares intensely at me, like he's waiting for me to commit.

"I don't even know where she is," I say.

"So we find out," Owen says, eyebrows raised.

"And then *Wreck* and *Ball*," Leo says, slapping his biceps and using this ridiculously bad MMA fighter voice, "will smash that jail apart!"

I can't help but laugh. "You can't be serious."

"This is as serious as I get." Owen holds out a hand. "Team Coyote?"

Leo slaps his hand on top of Owen's. "Team Coyote."

I drop my palm on top of theirs. "Team Coyote."

We pull into school so we drop our hands, but we share this secret smile. That makes it easier when Owen and Leo head over to the Champlain side, while I follow the Allen kids toward my locker. There's something holding us together, something bigger than seventh grade, something big enough to make even the sight of Taylor Mahoney approaching feel small.

"Dude, show him," Taylor grunts, shoving a kid with a phone in my face.

On the screen is a video — YouTube — and it's a mash-up of some cop show's credits and my school picture and footage from the fire. *"Gabe Meyer,"* says the voice in a terrible rap. *"He started the fire, though he tried to be a liar to save his butt."* I try to push past them, but the kid follows me, turns the volume up.

Another voice joins in on the clip. *"Gabe Meyer, got picked up by the cops and now is picking up trash with the rest of the crooks."*

Inside, I feel the earthquake start to rumble, the pressure building, the explosion coming. My fingernails dig into my palms, forming tight fists, tighter. But it's weird because it doesn't feel nearly as big as what I felt when they took my coyote.

I can handle this earthquake. I can breathe in and breathe out, and watch the pressure meter inside me go down. I can choose something other than exploding.

My mind moves on from the anger earthquake. And suddenly, the only thing that pops into my head is that the rap in this video is the worst rap I have ever heard. It doesn't rhyme, and the kid trying to beatbox in the background can't keep time to save his life. It is a terrible video.

These kids are hanging around me, waiting for me to

explode. I turn to face them. "Wow, Taylor, you learned how to use YouTube. Now, you just have to learn how to write a decent insult and keep time to music and maybe also how to sing and then you've got a real career option lined up." I pat the closest guy on the shoulder and then just walk away.

It feels so good, I almost run, smiling, down the rest of the hallway to my locker.

Some other people try to get me going with the video in homeroom, but I just laugh at the screen every time I see it. I mean, it is *that* bad. Why even make this video? It's not like anyone at the school doesn't know I started the fire.

On the fifth play of the video, I start writing better lyrics for it: *Gabriel Meyer / started a fire / burned up a chicken coop / and a chicken inside her.*

My pen stalls over the paper. Am I trying to set myself off?

But I don't go off. The little rumble? Nothing I can't handle. It makes me sad to think about Mr. Larkin's dead chicken, but sad is okay. And the anger, it's fizzling away, bubbles in soda, gone.

As soon as the morning announcements end, another kid— some guy I've never spoken to—starts playing the video under his desk as everyone shuffles around to leave homeroom, pointing at the screen so I can see it. He keeps glancing over his shoulder, waiting for me to throw a pencil or something. Did Taylor text this link to every kid in the school?

Out in the hallway, I hear, "Hey, Mey-ro the Pyro! I saw the video!"

"Aren't you special," I say, not even looking at whoever it is.

~

When I get to Rockledge that afternoon, I practically assault Zach for information.

"Have you heard anything about my coyote?"

Zach pushes me back a step. "Whoa! I'm throwing manure here. Don't push me into the poop!"

I laugh, step back. "Okay, so now, what do you know about my coyote?"

Zach's eyebrows shoot up. "You keep saying *your* coyote. A wild animal doesn't belong to anyone."

He's avoiding my question. Either he knows nothing for real or he knows something he doesn't want to tell me. "So she's dead?" My body freezes.

"Look, that animal was in pretty rough shape when we found her. I really don't know anything—I'm not a wildlife rehabber, I do trees. So you must chill. Focus on the work." He hands me his shovel. "We got a donation of a couple maple trees from a local gardening place. We need to throw some compost down to help them get started." He presses the shovel handle into my palm.

I grip the shovel. Take a deep breath. I squeeze the handle until my fingers turn white.

Zach grabs another shovel from the truck. "You know, you're the inspiration for this. The company who sent the trees mentioned seeing that a local kid was donating profits from his chicken coop sales to rebuild the picnic area."

My fingers relax. I dig my shovel into the pile, haul it to where Zach's tied up some surveyor's tape. "How could they know?"

"The company mentioned that one of their employees, a Paul Larkin, told them about it," Zach says, shoveling another pile onto the black dirt. "Name ring a bell? Anyway, the owner said they were happy to help."

I feel this smile lift the corner of my mouth. I inspired a company to donate some trees. Or I inspired Mr. Larkin to convince his company to donate some trees? Either way, I inspired someone to do something.

We shovel until the piles are gone and the trees are planted.

"I'm not sure I have much more work for you around here," Zach says.

"I can pull more buckthorn," I say. "I saw a serious baby buckthorn situation as I was coming in." I'm covered in sweat and my mind is empty. It feels good.

Zach nods. "Okay, we'll hit some invasives on Monday."

I take off my gloves, stuff them in my backpack. And jammed in the bottom is the food I should have dropped off the other day for my girl. A lump stops in my throat. "Zach, do you think that if the animal control people make my coyote better, they might decide to just let her live?"

Zach hefts the last of the tools into the truck. "That's beyond my pay grade," he says. "I mean, Fish and Wildlife has a public relations problem because of this coyote. People don't really like coyotes to begin with, but if they're just living their coyote lives, the wardens can tell people to leave them alone. But once a coyote makes a name for itself—if it moves into someone's yard or is attacking their livestock or, in this case, bites a kid—the warden has less room to tell people to just try to get along with the wildlife."

The anger swells up hearing Zach talk about this stuff like it's not my coyote's life he's discussing. She's going to die—that's a little more than a "public relations" problem. Liz declared herself my "public relations" manager for my chicken coops, and then started blathering on about the "urban chicken market" and the need for the coops to have a cool paint job. Public relations is just selling something. Like Taylor was trying to sell me as the lone fire-starter in that stupid video.

And then it clicks. What if I made a video about the fire and about my coyote? I could tell people my coyote's side of the story. Maybe I could find and interview the family, see if the kid who got bitten is okay. If I could get people to see that she's not a threat, or that she was only a threat because of how scared she was, maybe the game warden will have second thoughts?

Problems need solutions, as Mr. Larkin said—this could be the solution to the warden's public relations problem.

"Zach, you're a genius!"

"What now?"

"I'll see you Monday!"

I bike by Mr. Larkin's house—I want to thank him for talking to his boss about the park—and he asks if he can come over this Sunday to help build more coops. I tell him only if he brings his staple gun, and he laughs, but says he will—score!

I bike home fast, hoping to catch Owen before dinner. I find him shooting goals on his front lawn. "Hey," I say. "Nice shot."

He wipes his forehead on his wristband. "Thanks."

"You have a second?"

He picks up his ball, comes to the edge of the lawn. "What's up?"

I tell him what Zach said about my—well, our—coyote's "public relations" problem. And then I'm like, "You saw the video Taylor made, right?" I play it on my phone.

Owen's face scrunches as he watches. "Taylor made that video? That kid is the worst."

"It shows in the video. I mean, you heard how terrible the rap is?"

"Point taken," Owen says, tipping his head at me.

I explain my plan. "If a fart-brain like Taylor can make a video, just imagine how great the video we make will be."

Owen's on his phone, texting. "Leo will love this."

"Meet at my place tomorrow? We can use my Mom's laptop." I hope this is true.

"Yeah," he says. "We'll come by after the game."

"Cool."

I bike home, and it's so weird to be coming from this direction, from Owen's house. It feels good. Like old times. Or even better than old times, because we've been through something together. We're not just friends because we happen to live a block apart and go to the same school. We're friends now because we chose to be. That's cooler than before.

TWENTY-SEVEN
Rill

LIGHT SPARKS ON outside the box I'm trapped inside. There are false suns in this room, long bars of light that flick on and off at the human's touch. I lift my head, check beyond the shiny twigs that hold me in. A human has come into the room.

The other animals begin to make their noises—squeaks, squeals, cries, yips, birdcalls of all sorts.

The human is joined by other humans. The box is terrible, but the humans feed me, like the other human did in the cave. These humans, however, also cover my muzzle with a tube that makes me sleepy. When I woke the first time, I found that they had wrapped my paws in these cushiony webs. I had a long vine coming from my leg. At first, I was too exhausted to fight any of these things. But in the days since, I have grown stronger.

Yesterday, I defeated the vine in my leg. Last night, I removed one of the webs from my paw.

The strangest thing is that the webs seem to have fixed my paws. My pads don't hurt nearly as much. Were the vines helping, too? My insides feel better.

A human approaches my box, and I growl a warning, "Stay back."

The human opens the twigs just a crack. I growl louder, "Stay away!"

The human reaches in with a pole and string and wraps it around my neck, then pulls me out swiftly into its arms, holding my head against its shoulder.

"Release me!" I yip, wiggling with all my strength.

A second human sticks the tube over my muzzle, and the air becomes sweet and I am sleepy, oh so sleepy . . .

~

I awaken now on a flat stone floor. In front of me is dirt, real dirt! And trees. Am I home?

I lift my nose, scent the air.

No, not home.

The stone floor connects to stone walls and one of those false suns shines over me. But in front of my paws there is nothing but dirt, strange dirt, but dirt, nonetheless. I dare to try to stand. My paws hold me, my legs, too. There's no pain.

I step forward onto the dirt, feel the soft grains against my paw pads, and joy spreads through me. I can walk. My legs wobble—I haven't walked in nearly a moon. It takes several tries, but I manage a few steps without wobbling, and then a lope.

My way is blocked by hard, thin, interwoven twigs. The dirt goes on, but I cannot follow it.

So I am not home, nor am I free. I am trapped, only the box is bigger.

I sniff along the woven wall of twigs. The wall extends in all directions, except for the part that is the stone wall with the false light. There are trees and rocks and sticks around. It is a false forest to match the false suns.

Near one large tree, there's a nook created by a rock and a log. I curl myself into it and try not to think about what happens next. Will the humans let me go back to my forest? Will I ever find Teeth again? What hope is there of finding my family now?

A growl rises up inside me, an anger at these humans. They have fixed my paws, but for what? To live alone in this false world?

I must wait. I must watch. I am still wobbly on my paws, so I must get stronger. And once I am, I will find a way out of this place, a way home.

TWENTY-EIGHT

Gabe

THE SECOND I WAKE UP, I rewatch the video. Yesterday, Owen, Leo, and I cut together a bunch of news footage about the fire and some clips we found of coyotes in the wild, but it's not selling the idea of saving my girl. Coyotes are viewed as problems in urban areas when they're healthy and leave everyone alone. Coyotes who bite? Bad news. So we've got to try something different. The question is, what?

I get dressed and head downstairs. And discover my dad and Mr. Larkin just hanging out, drinking coffee.

"There he is," Dad says, pointing his mug at me.

Mr. Larkin looks over his shoulder. "Morning, Gabe."

Oh, right! He's coming to help build more coops today. "Hey, Mr. Larkin. You got here early."

"Is eight early?" He looks to my dad, smiling wryly.

"It is for seventh-graders." Dad gets up, checks something on the stove. "We have sausages. Paul, can I sell you a couple?"

"I'm buying if you're selling."

I realize quickly that they have been sitting here, talking, for over an hour. And that my dad looks happier and less twitchy than normal.

"I'll take a few," I say, grabbing plates and silverware.

Liz appears on the stairs. "Do I smell sausage?" She takes a fork and picks one straight out of the pan. "What were you and the soccer twins doing yesterday?" she asks, plopping herself down at the table. Liz took her SAT test yesterday and ever since has been a lot less grumpy.

"Making a video about my coyote," I say, sliding into the last chair. "Here," I say, handing her my phone with the clip.

"Gabe is worried about this coyote from the fire," Dad explains to Mr. Larkin. "He's trying to save it from Fish and Wildlife."

"The one that they said bit my neighbor's kid?" Mr. Larkin says. "Not sure that cow can be milked."

"If anyone can milk that cow, it's me," I say. "She's not a bad coyote. She was just scared. Because of what I did." I have to squeeze the last words out, but I say them.

Mr. Larkin sips his coffee. "I hear you. But people have a bad idea about coyotes."

"Time was, coyotes were considered vermin," Dad says.

"When I was a kid, my friends would go out on coyote-hunting contests, with a prize for whoever took out the most."

I feel the rumbles of anger rising in me. "But they live here, too. My girl had every right to be in that forest. She only bit that kid because she was scared of the fire. I took care of her for weeks and she never attacked me."

"She was sick and trapped in a cave," Liz adds, looking up from my phone. "She might have wanted to attack you."

"No," I say. "She's good. She doesn't deserve to be put down."

Mr. Larkin swallows, wipes his mouth on his napkin. "You could talk to the family. They are real animal lovers, far as I can tell."

"You think they might talk to the game warden?" I ask, this bubble of hope inflating inside me.

He shrugs. "You could ask."

Liz puts down my phone, goes to get herself coffee—gross. At what age does coffee suddenly taste good to people? "I think you need an Instagram and Twitter feed for this project. That would get the word out to a bigger audience, to put some pressure on the warden from outside. Maybe Facebook, too, and connect it all with a basic website."

The hope bubble deflates. "I barely got a two-minute video clip together in a day," I say. "How long will all that take?"

Liz waves her hand. "I'll do it. It'll take, like, five seconds."

A part of me is like, *Perfect, done,* but another part recalls the difference between helping and just doing it for someone. "Can you show me how to do it?"

Liz's eyebrows go up, impressed. "Okay."

But Mr. Larkin's here . . . "Maybe this afternoon?"

"We'll start on the coops," Dad says to me. "You and Liz do your thing."

"I'll be out as soon as I'm finished," I say.

I shove the last few bites of sausage into my mouth and follow Liz up to her room.

~

Liz teaches me some basics of social media and website design, and by lunchtime, we've built a digital empire for my girl. Liz leaves to help at the football practice, but Owen and Leo stop by after their soccer game, and the five of us manage to get one entire coop built by sundown. My dad and Mr. Larkin have really hit it off, which is kind of weird but cool.

"Paul, let me walk you out," Dad says, wiping his hands on his work pants.

"All right, Joe," Mr. Larkin says.

"I like the orange paint," Owen says as Leo finishes the door. "It says, *Chickens*."

"It says pumpkins if it says anything." Leo drops his brush into the water bucket.

"Chickens like pumpkins." Owen shoves Leo in the shoulder.

"More important? I think it'll sell for a hundred bucks easy,"

I say, already mentally adding the money into my park fund. "Now, back to our coyote campaign. The video is not enough."

"Time for a prison break?" Leo says, slapping a wet brush on his palm.

"Seriously," I say. "When I started that fire—"

"When *we* started the fire," Owen corrects.

Leo bursts into some song about not starting a fire, drumming with the wet brushes and spraying water.

"Dude," Owen says.

"What even is that?" I ask.

"Billy Joel? Hello? Nothing? You guys don't know good music."

"Billy Joel is grandma music." Owen flings a little chunk of wood at Leo.

"Billy Joel is an American classic."

"That's what your grandma said," I add.

"Shut up, Allen," Leo says, chucking the same little piece of wood.

"Eat it, Champlain Classic," I say, chucking it back, and then it's a tiny-wood-piece-chucking battle for like five minutes before I can get everyone focused again on the topic at hand: "So, coyotes."

"Right," Owen says.

"We need to get that family with that kid to ask to save the coyote," I say.

"What?" Leo says. "No way those people will be on the coyote's side of this situation."

I shrug. "Mr. Larkin knows them. He thinks they might. They're apparently animal nuts."

"The kid," says Owen, slinging a finger like he's hitting the point on a map. "If we get the kid on our side, the parents will be on our side."

"You want to manipulate a little kid?" Leo asks, and I am kind of with him on this one.

"No," Owen says, "well, yeah. But, like, what if we did a presentation or something at the elementary school?"

"I think that kid was too little for elementary school," says Leo. "In the video, she looked, like, tiny."

And it hits me. "Next weekend is the Harvest Festival at Charlotte Farms. That place is crawling with little kids. We could ask about doing a table or something. About coyotes."

"We could ask the science museum if we could borrow their furs," Leo suggests. "The museum is always out there with furs, and my little brother is all over those things."

"And crafts, or face painting," Owen says.

"This festival thing is good," Leo says. "This will work."

"We hit them with good coyote vibes at the festival," I say, "and then go to the house and interview them."

"Add it to our video?" Owen asks.

"No, another video," I say. "Liz and I made a social media empire for us."

"Dude, we'll be coyote *influencers*," Leo says, spreading his arms out as if creating our empire.

"That's not a thing," Owen says.

"We'll make it a thing," I say.

Owen smiles. "Okay," he says. "You're the boss."

"The boss of sawdust," Leo says, and the wood starts flying.

~

"You need a hashtag," Liz says, waving her toast around Monday morning. "*Save the coyote* or something with 'coyote' in it."

"It needs to be specific," Mom offers, peering up from her newspaper. "Maybe *Save the Rockledge coyote*?"

"That's too long," Liz says.

"I like it," Dad says, smiling at Mom and bringing a pile of scrambled eggs to the table.

We all agreed to wake up a half-hour earlier on weekdays to avoid the "morning tangle," as Mom called it, and so far it seems to be working.

"*Rockledge coyotes rock*," I say, spreading my hands like I'm revealing a marquee.

Liz nods approvingly. "That's what I'm talking about."

I pull out my phone and add the hashtag to our social media, then shovel the eggs into my mouth. I have another coop to start after school, plus I have to call the science museum and see about borrowing their fur . . .

Dad pulls off Mom's old apron and hangs it on a hook near the door to the basement. "Well, I've got to run. I have an appointment at Mill's Gardening Center." He turns, checks his tie—he's wearing a tie?—in the glass front of the microwave. "An *interview*."

Now we all sit up straight.

"A what?" Mom asks, paper now folded on the table.

Dad glances back over his shoulder, obviously glad to see his little show has had its intended effect. "Paul—Paul Larkin? —he tipped me off that they had a purchase and sales opening at the place where he works. He's semiretired, so he's not interested, but he gave me the owner's number, said to use his name, and so yesterday afternoon I did. Me and this guy—Mr. Mills—hit it off, and he told me to come in for an interview. It's the off-season, but he said they do a brisk business during the holidays."

Mom looks like she's been hit with a bat.

"That's great, Dad," Liz says, standing to give him a hug.

"Yeah," I say, and get up because I guess that's what we should do.

"They're hiring in sales?" Mom mumbles from her chair. "And it's a full-time, salaried position?"

"With commissions," Dad says, waggling his eyebrows now. Who is this man and why is he dressed like my dad?

Mom is practically in tears. She jumps up and hugs him.

He laughs, pushes her off, but he's obviously in heaven. "It's just an interview, but I feel good about it."

They start talking about serious things like budgets and numbers, which is my cue to get to the bus. But it's nice to see my dad happy. I hadn't really thought about it, but he's been in a bad mood for months. Maybe years. Even before he lost his job. And that bad mood kind of wormed its way into the house, into each one of us. I remember last year, around Passover, he jumped down Mom's throat about the brisket, and we were all just frozen — MaMa and PopPop, me and Liz, Grandma Meyer — afraid to stick up for her and afraid to attack him. We kind of just kept eating, pretended it didn't happen, and hoped the bad mood would go away.

I guess things were getting bad at Dad's job then; he lost it a few weeks later. When Mom got her job, even though that was huge, he seemed almost angrier about it. Everything made him angrier. He *was* his bad mood. And we were all caught in it.

Now that it's lifted — it's been lifting for weeks, really — I can see it for what it was. For how I felt that bad mood inside me. How I've been my own bad mood. But that it's been lifting, too.

There's no guarantee it won't be back. My dad might not get this job. Things might be bad again for me in school or in life. But I'm different—the same, but stronger. Like with Owen and Leo—we're the same, but different, better. Maybe it's the same for my family. Maybe we're stronger now. Maybe the next time a bad mood storm hits, we'll find a way to come together instead of tearing each other apart.

~

On Wednesday, I get a private message on Instagram to the public coyote account. *I'm the Mom who called Fish and Wildlife. Please message me back.*

I find Owen and Leo after school. "What do I do?" I ask, holding the phone screen toward them.

"Message her back?" Owen says, shrugging.

"And say what?" I feel like I'm holding a bomb that's about to go off.

"Tell her what you want," Leo says. "Tell her you found the coyote, and she was injured, and that that's why she bit her kid, and that you're trying to save her."

"That's it?" It seems too easy.

Leo nods. "Dude, she saw your Insta, she knows what you're about. If she's contacting you, it means she's on your side, or at least is interested."

When I get to Rockledge, before I meet up with Zach, I

message her back, tell her I would really like to talk to her. By the time I've finished my hours and am heading out to bike home, I have an email.

> *Hi Gabe,*
>
> *Thank you for replying to my message. I don't know if you remember, but I was at your community justice panel. We were really shaken by the fire, and how close it came to our home. When that coyote came out and snapped at my daughter, it just broke me. But I didn't realize that the Fish and Wildlife Department would put the animal down.*
>
> *I called the Fish and Wildlife Department after your panel and told them that I didn't want them to put the coyote down. I explained that my daughter was fine and didn't have to even get a rabies shot—there was no actual bite! But they have a policy about nuisance coyotes, especially injured nuisance coyotes. They told me it was a set policy.*
>
> *Please let me know if there's anything I can do to help.*

I put some stuff about nuisance animals on the website, mostly links to animal welfare organizations' pages about how these predators are an essential part of the ecosystem and better ways to manage wildlife-human encounters. But coyotes are generally viewed as bad guys. They eat people's livestock in the country, and knock over trash cans and scare people's dogs in the city. But they don't want to hurt people. It's not like the coyote means to eat your particular prized sheep or attack your expensive composter. It's just a coyote being a coyote, living its wild life.

How do you get people to like something that's kind of a pain in the neck?

Worse, is it even about that anymore? If the lady who called the Fish and Wildlife people can't get them to change their minds, what can I do?

I feel the anger begin to rumble inside. I want to bike to wherever they're holding my girl and bust her out with my fists. I pedal home hard, try to channel all that anger into my feet.

I show the email to Owen and Leo while we do some before-dinner coop work. "I feel like it's hopeless," I say, smashing a nail into the wood. "If this lady couldn't get them to save her, what can we do? It's like after everything, no matter what I do, my girl's going to die because of me. And for no good reason."

"Take it out on the wood," Owen says.

Leo nods.

I nail the rest of the frame together in five solid whacks.

At dinner, Liz tries to make me feel better. "Gabe, you just have to keep going with the social media. It's like you said — the coyote is a public relations problem. If you give the Fish and Wildlife Department another public relations problem, a pro-coyote public relations problem, they'll have to change their minds."

Mom puts a hand on my arm. "Listen, buddy, I agree with Liz, but we also have to recognize that this is bigger than you and this one coyote. If there's a policy, there's a reason for that policy."

The anger boils up, but I hold it. I take a deep breath. "It's a bad policy," I manage to say.

Dad drops some plates into the sink and starts rinsing. "Sometimes you just have to accept that bad things happen." He's still waiting to hear about the job, so he's right on the edge of a bad mood.

Liz shoves me in the shoulder. "It's not over," she says. "We have to look forward to the festival."

The farm has decided to let us do our booth at the festival, and to combine it with some of their resources on alternatives to traps, poisons, and hunting to manage predators and live-stock encounters. Llamas apparently scare coyotes and are used on sheep farms to protect the flocks. I've never found llamas particularly scary, but hey, if it works.

"Right," I say, and try to tell the same thing to the anger: *It's not over, there's still something to be done.*

~

Mom picks up the coyote fur on her way home from work Thursday. It's really soft—I can see why people would want this for a coat. But then I think of my girl, and that this could have been her fur, and the anger shakes my bones.

Friday, I spend every minute I'm not in class working on a handout for the festival. The librarian helps me get the layout just right. Mrs. Dooley catches me working on it during math lab, and she just shakes her head and lets me keep going.

Mrs. Dooley's all right.

At Rockledge that afternoon, Zach can tell I'm distracted. "What's going on with you this week? You're barely staying over your assigned hours."

I laugh. "Sorry, but I've got a lot going on."

He leans on his rake. "I saw your website. It inspired me to pull some strings, and I managed to get some info out of the rehab center. The coyote's still there and is even recovering."

My heart rate jumps to track-star speeds. "She's better?"

He goes back to raking. "That's the word."

"She's better," I whisper to myself as I scratch a patch of dirt clear of leaf litter, then rip out a buckthorn shoot hiding underneath.

"The fact that they even put her in rehab is a good sign," he continues. "Either they don't know for sure she's the coyote that bit the kid, or maybe they're having second thoughts."

It's too much to hope for. "Do you really think so?"

He tips his head. "My contact said the normal protocol

would have been to euthanize the coyote on arrival. I think this is a good sign."

"I'll take it," I say, and rake like I've never raked before. Apparently, hope gives you way more energy than anger.

After I finish, Dad picks me up, and we drive by the house where the lady whose kid got snapped at by my coyote lives. She offered to make a little testimonial about the incident for our website. Dad offered to film me talking to her.

We start in the backyard and the lady—Mrs. Fischer—explains to me how she could see the fire through the trees, and then the coyote was there, in their yard, and their daughter toddled over to it.

"It all happened so fast, and all at once. My daughter and I were more scared than hurt."

She adds a plea for the coyote's life without my even asking her to. At the end, she shakes my hand. "I think it's great you're trying to save this animal."

"It's kind of my fault she's in trouble," I say.

Mrs. Fischer shrugs. "A lot of kids would say 'it's not my problem.' I like that you're making it your problem."

We say goodbye, and I meet Dad at the car. "Thanks," I say, getting in.

"My pleasure," he says, idly swiping his phone. "You did a great job. I'm impressed. Really, Gabe, I'm impressed with everything you've done. You really *repaired the harm*." He smiles at me.

Hearing that from my dad—I don't know how to respond. This blush flushes my face. Before I can say anything, his phone dings.

He jumps, looks at it nervously.

"You want me to check it?" I ask.

"Nah," he says. "Let's not ruin the moment."

When he finally checks it after dinner, he is barely able to get out the announcement: he got the job. We're all so psyched, we go out for ice cream to celebrate like it's years ago and I'm five, but, man, that ice cream tastes so good.

~

Early Saturday morning, Liz drives Owen, Leo, and me over to Charlotte Farms to prepare for the festival. A table has been set up for us, and we put out the coyote pelt and the stack of handouts I printed at school. I also have a petition—Mrs. Dooley's suggestion—for people to sign to save my coyote.

Leo lays out some face paints he found in his house for us to draw noses and whiskers on kids' faces.

"Okay," Liz says, letting the measuring tape zip back into its holder. "I've measured thirteen feet in the grass over there and marked it with spray paint. Kids can see if they can jump as far as a coyote. We can also time them with this"—she pulls out a stopwatch—"that I borrowed from the team's bag—don't tell—to see how fast they can run and compare that to the coyote's forty-three miles per hour."

This is so much cooler than anything I imagined.

I walk up to Liz and hug her. "Thank you," I manage.

She slings one arm around me. "I'm in this, too, bro."

The day is long and chilly, but we paint a lot of faces. Kids love petting the coyote fur. Liz's coyote challenges are so popular, we have to organize the kids into lines. Over a hundred parents sign my petition.

That night, I scan the sheet and all the signatures into a PDF and begin my email to the warden.

> *Dear Sir,*
> *I am the boy who started the fire in Rockledge Park.*

I have to be up front about that.

> *I am writing to ask that you change your decision about the coyote who scared that little kid during the fire. I talked to the lady who complained about the coyote, Mrs. Fischer, and she said that the coyote didn't even bite her kid.*

I feel like this is my best argument: The crime was never even committed!

*I have spoken to other people in the community, and they sup-
port saving the coyote. They all signed a petition saying so. A scan
of the petition is attached to this email.*

There's the public relations pressure.

*The coyote is not a bad animal. Coyotes are native predators
here in Vermont. This coyote has a right to live in Rockledge Park.
It wasn't her fault that she got scared by the fire. It was my fault.
Please don't hold her responsible for my mistake.*

And there's the truth.

*Yours truly,
Gabriel Meyer*

I read it over a couple of times, make sure I didn't spell anything wrong. I attach the scan of the petition. I hit send.

Please work, I beg God or the universe or whatever is listening. *Please let this change the warden's mind.*

Twenty-nine

Rill

THE TRUE SUN GLINTS above the tree line and warms my fur. I stand, stretch—first back, lowering my snout almost to the dirt, then forward, extending each of my legs and wiggling my toes. I lope around the perimeter of the false forest I am trapped inside. I can make it around in seventy heartbeats, which is fifty heartbeats faster than when I was first placed in here.

Why are the humans keeping me trapped here? If they were caging me to fix me, how do I tell them I'm fixed? Obviously, they have to figure that out for themselves. But they haven't even checked on me in suns.

Grrr, I am so BORED. I want to hunt, to feel my paws in the soft dirt between the trees, to smell the scent of a marmot as it peeks from its hole. I want to run as far and as long as I want.

I want to swim and dig and play and—oh my fur, I've turned into my siblings.

I snuffle a laugh. All it took was a fire, nearly dying, and being rescued by humans and healed in a box to make me feel it: a desire to play that smothers everything else.

I lost that feeling long before the end of my puppyhood, when my brothers were taken from me. Mother and Father changed then, too—they were always watchful, always barking at me to stay close, keep alert. There could be no fun because fun was what took you from them. I understand why they felt that, and why they feared for the runts, and why they were so hard on me. But their fear was just that: fear.

I hope their fear did not turn on Teeth. I hope, when I return to the forest, he can lead me to them and I can fight the fear inside my parents and free us all from its curse. Then, maybe, we can all play together, becoming a cloud of dust that sparkles in the sun.

~

The little flap in the stone wall opens and meat slides into the enclosure. I trot over and begin to eat—I'm not terribly hungry, but there's food. I might as well eat it.

This food tastes a little different. There are these kind of foul-tasting grits.

Bleh!

Why put grits in with perfectly good meat? I eat the rest of the bites.

My head feels funny.

I shake my head and stumble slightly. What is wrong with me?

Water, I need water.

I drink. I drink and drink and drink . . .

There's this cloudy feeling in my head, like everything's covered in cobwebs. Why can't I put my feet one in front of the other? I'm tripping over my own paws.

"What's happening?" I whimper.

I can't feel my paws. I can't feel my whiskers. My rump hits the dirt. I didn't tell it to hit the dirt. Now I'm all in the dirt. I can't lift my head.

Help! But I can't even howl the cry. My snout is still, my eyelids slide down, my breathing slows, and all goes black.

THIRTY

Gabe

MONDAY MORNING, AFTER FIRST PERIOD, I check my phone and there's an email from a game warden.

> *Dear Gabriel,*
>
> *Thank you for your email. I appreciate your care and concern for the Rockledge coyote. Raising awareness about the role of predators in our ecosystem is an important step in their conservation. However, there are many factors that go into our decisions concerning nuisance animals. I assure you that we will carefully weigh all options in our management of local wildlife.*

At lunch, I find Leo and Owen. "Look at this non-answer answer." I hold out my phone to them.

"*Carefully weigh all options?* What options?" Owen says.

I shrug. "It's either release or murder as far as I know."

"No," says Leo. "We are going to have to hit them with even more public relations pressure."

"We made a petition," I say. "What else is there?"

Leo throws up his hands. "I don't know. Skywriting?"

"I'm pretty sure that's beyond the budget," I say. The anger is rumbling somewhere behind my navel.

Owen kicks a chunk of pavement. "This bites."

The other kids are just running around, playing basketball or four square. Cora and her gang are sitting on top of the half-wall next to the stairs gossiping. If we could get *them* to gang up on the Fish and Wildlife Department, there's no way the wardens wouldn't cave.

"That's it," I say, pushing myself off the wall.

"What's *it*?" asks Leo.

"Cora Phillips," I say. "She's the start, but then, like, everyone. If we get everyone in the school on this, maybe they'll get their parents on it, and they'll get the whole community on it, and *boom*. The game warden has no choice but to free our coyote."

"You think you can get Cora Phillips to even talk to you after the garbage can incident?" Leo asks.

"That was not my fault."

"Your fault or not, she's not exactly Gabe Meyer's biggest fan."

"Okay," I say, teeth gritted, "then you guys talk to her. Didn't she have a crush on you, Leo?"

"In fourth grade, maybe." He waves it off, but I can tell he's still into the idea.

"He can push that angle," Owen says, smiling. "I'll help."

A flicker of hope pushes into the cloud of anger in my gut. "Right," I say. "And I'll text Liz. Get her working in the high school. Maybe I can also get the teachers?"

Owen holds a hand out, palm down. "Team Coyote," he says.

Leo and I slap our hands over his.

"Go!" we shout together.

~

Mrs. Dooley is my best and only option. After a quick pitch between classes, she agrees to hang a poster about our project in the teacher's lounge. I tell Owen and Leo after school when they meet me at the bike stand. "How about you guys?" I ask.

"They're in," Leo says.

"Who's in?" I ask, afraid to hear the answer I know is coming.

"Cora, Ophelia, the whole gang," Owen says. "I told her the coyote is like a cute wild dog, and her eyes just went—" He mimes eyes exploding open.

"It's a lie," I say, a little uncomfortable with his tactics. "Coyotes attack pet dogs."

Leo cuts a hand across his throat. "Dude, ix-nay on the attack-yay." He swings his chin, and I see Cora approaching.

She walks up to Leo, gives me a flash of side-eye. "I called my uncle and he says he's in."

"That's amazing," Leo says, holding a hand up for a high-five, which she ignores.

"What's amazing?" I snap.

Cora turns the full weight of her gaze on me. "My uncle works as a producer at WGMZ. I pitched your story to him and he's interested."

"What's the catch?" I ask, because I know there's a catch.

"He thinks it's *my* school project," she says. "So I have to be at the filming."

Before I can get the *nuh* of *no way* started, Owen cuts a hand across my chest. "That's cool," he says. "Thanks."

Cora squints at me. "I'll text you the deets," she says to Leo, and walks off.

"She is the worst," I say.

"She is helping us majorly," Leo says. "She got us a news feature!"

"It's exactly the signal boost we need," Owen says.

I shrug. "I have to get to my community service," I say, hopping onto my bike.

"This is a good thing," Owen yells after me. I hope he's right . . .

~

As I'm biking over to the park, my phone rings, so I stop to check who it is, and it's Ms. Andrews.

"Hi, Gabe!" she says, way too happy as usual. "I just wanted to touch base because Zach emailed me over your hours and you are way over forty, kiddo. You completed your service a week or so ago. So we can schedule your exit meeting."

My brain gets stuck on what she's said. It's over. For some reason, this actually makes me some mixture of nervous and sad. "Oh, great," I manage to say.

"I'm really proud of you, Gabe. Zach said you worked harder than anyone he's worked with on trail maintenance. He also said you've taken on extra service work for the park?"

"Oh, the chicken coops?" I ask. "Yeah, well, I wanted to actually fix the park, you know, so it would be like it was." I then add, "As much as it can be, I mean. I know it will never be the same after what I did."

"I think it's great." I can hear a smile in her voice.

It suddenly occurs to me that Ms. Andrews might have some sway with the game wardens. "I'm also trying to save that coyote who was in the fire, the one that allegedly bit the kid. You know, the mom says her daughter wasn't even really bitten."

"Oh, wow," she says on the other end of the line. "Well, that's a great project, too."

Her voice is different now, a little hesitant. "It is," I assure her. "I've got a website and social media campaign, and we did a booth at the Harvest Festival last weekend. My friends and I might even get a news guy to cover it."

"That's all fantastic, Gabe. I just found your page online—this is really amazing." I hear her typing and clicking. "I just—" She pauses. "Gabe, you know that this is bigger than just you and your friends, right? Wildlife management is complicated, and especially with nuisance animals—"

"Yeah, I know," I snap. It's taking all my effort to control the anger that's boiling up.

"I know you know," she says, voice calm, steady. "But have you prepared yourself for what happens if you can't save this particular coyote?"

My words die in my throat. No, I haven't prepared myself for that at all. I am not prepared to fail. I can't fail. It's my fault she's in trouble, it's my fault, mine, mine . . .

"Gabe?" Ms. Andrews asks.

"It's going to work," I say, voice cracking at the end.

"But what if it doesn't, Gabe? Do you have a plan for yourself if this is something you can't fix?"

It's weird hearing her say it, but I know it's true. I need a plan for if this doesn't work or I'll just explode. I've seen it with the fire, with my dad, with myself. This is something out of my control, a decision I can't make, and I have pinned my whole self to it working out okay. What will I do if it doesn't?

"What kind of plan?" I ask her.

"You need to find something that will work for you. Maybe it's about continuing to raise awareness about coyotes. Maybe it's volunteering with a wildlife rehabilitation group. Maybe it's just making peace with this being out of your control, and that you've done all you can to save the coyote."

"How I am supposed to make peace with my coyote dying for no good reason, all because of what I did?"

"The way we have to make peace with anything that's beyond our control," she says. "By accepting what we can do, the kinds of things you've already done to help this coyote, and also accepting that there are things we can't do, like ensure that this particular coyote gets released."

If I can't save my coyote, I could get angry. I could rage and complain and spread my bad mood over the whole world. I could go so far as to start sending hate mail to the wardens, attacking animal control people—there are so many ways I could try to burn it all down.

But I've tried it that way. And it only made me feel worse. Alone, and angry, and tired, and sad, and scared . . .

"Okay," I say.

"Okay what?" she asks.

"You're right. I have to accept that this is out of my control."

And just saying it, there's this little lift in my chest. Not like I've given up on my girl, but that I've loosened my grip on the idea that it's all on me.

"You're a great kid, Gabe," Ms. Andrews says. "I really hope you can."

"Me, too," I say.

We hang up, and I bike the rest of the way to the park, going back and forth over it in my mind. Every time I tell myself, *I'm doing all I can to save my coyote and it's out of my control,* there's this other voice inside that's like, *You should call more people, make posters, protest in front of the State House.* Like any one of these moves is the one that will save my girl.

I meet Zach at our stump. He stands when he sees me, arms open wide. "Here's the conquering hero! Did the justice center call you? I put in your hours—you're done! Up high!" He holds his palm up for me to slap.

I touch it weakly. "Yeah, they called."

"Dude, what's going on?"

I tell him about what Ms. Andrews said.

"Whoa," he says, slumping down onto the stump. "That's a lot."

"Yeah," I say, sitting next to him.

"But you know she's right, right?"

"Yeah," I say. I kick a rock, and it rolls into a pile of leaves.

He kicks a pebble, and it rolls past mine, down the trail. "It's like with rock climbing," he says. "When I face a wall, I have to pick my route really carefully. I try to plan for every hold, every place I put my foot. But in the end, I can only control so much. Maybe the rock is slippery with a little moisture from the air, maybe my hand is sweaty and my finger grip slides. No matter how well I plan, there's a chance I end up hanging from my rope.

"But that's the point of the rope, Gabe. You do your best, or sometimes you just mess up and something bad happens, and you've got to have something holding you up. You don't want to just free fall every time you slip."

The wind rustles the leaves overhead. A few fall, helicoptering down to the forest floor. I can't let go of my girl. I can't stop trying.

What's my rope?

Zach slaps my shoulder. "Let's hit those invasives." He stands and pulls two rakes and a bucket out of the back of the truck.

I grab mine, and we work until we're both sweating and the bucket is full.

After we put the rakes away, Zach holds out his hand. "Good work, dude."

I shake his palm, the dirt on both our gloves rubbing off and falling in a shower. "Thanks."

"I'll miss having a helper every day."

"I'd like to keep helping," I say. "If it's okay with you?"

Zach nods. "I'll be moving around East Burlington, though. You and I have set this place back on track. Now, I have to give some love to my other parks."

"I can bike anywhere in town."

He smiles. "Nice. Welcome aboard, junior forester."

~

Cora catches up with me in the hallway at school. "My uncle says we need to have a segment with the park to bring in the fire aspect of the story. I heard that you . . . work there. Could you ask if we can film there?"

Her voice is like feedback squeal to my ears: I can't help but cringe. "Fine," I say.

Cora frowns. "I'm sorry, Gabe," she says quietly. "About coming up to you that day. I didn't think about how hard it must have been for you, being at school, after everything."

I'm so shocked, I just stare at her for a second. "Um, okay. Thanks?"

She turns to go.

"I'm sorry, too," I say quickly. She stops. "I didn't mean to spill all that garbage on you. I just snapped."

She nods her head. "See you Wednesday."

~

At community service—though I guess it's not really that anymore, just service to the community that I'm volunteering—I ask Zach about featuring the park in the news story and if he'd talk about what we've done to restore it for the local wildlife.

"Sure, dude," he says. "Anything." He then puts a hand on my shoulder. "You got that rope on, though, right?"

I nod. But I don't yet.

Owen pitches adding an interview with the mom of the alleged coyote victim, and Cora's uncle loves the idea. I call Mrs. Fischer to see if she'll participate. She's excited, says she's proud of me, for everything I've done.

"It might not be enough," I tell her.

"Oh, I'm sure this news story will do the trick!"

I don't argue with her, but after we hang up, I keep thinking, *No, it might not*. It's weird that a grownup would say that. Doesn't she know that this isn't something I can control?

Maybe this is one of those times when grownups try to pretend everything's going to be okay when maybe it's not. Maybe it's just easier to say, *This is the clincher*, than admit there's no such thing. That you can work, and try, and put in every last bit of effort you can think of, and still fail.

Wednesday, Leo and Owen skip a drills practice, and the three of us bike over to the park. Cora shows up with her uncle and his film crew, and we set up in the burned area. Cora interviews Zach about the park's wildlife and recovery efforts after the fire, then talks to Owen, Leo, and me about our efforts to save the Rockledge coyote. We leave out my days of caring for her in secret on Mom's advice—the whole CJC thing is meant to stay confidential—and make out like this was a cause we stumbled upon. At Mrs. Fischer's house, Cora really turns on the charm and gets an awesome interview about the incident. Mrs. Fischer even feels inspired to make a pitch about wanting to save this coyote, and that the whole thing was a misunderstanding. Everyone's excited, slapping each other's hands, and I feel it, too: a sense that this is the clincher, that we've done it, that my girl is saved. But as we bike home, doubt creeps back in.

~

Thursday night, we watch the news story over dinner. Afterward, my dad slaps me on the shoulder. "That's pretty incredible."

"I'm so proud of you, Gabe," Mom says.

"I hope it's enough," Liz says.

I take a deep breath. "We've done all we can," I say.

Everyone looks at me, shocked and slightly stunned.

I shrug. "I'm being realistic. Now, we have to wait and see if it works."

"And if it doesn't?" my mom asks. There's a tremble in her voice: her fear that this will knock me down so hard I won't be able to get back up again.

"If it doesn't," I say, "at least I know I did everything I could to save her." I'm trying the words on for size, flexing myself inside them.

My parents look at me like they don't quite know me, but in

a good way, like they're surprised to find that their ugly duckling was a swan all along.

"You did," Liz says, squeezing my arm.

"You did," Mom says.

"If they don't save this coyote," Dad adds, "we're writing a letter to our congressman."

We go back to eating, talking, and I realize that maybe this is the rope: That my family is back together. That my friends are back. That I have different friends all over town that I care about.

Maybe the rope is the caring. It's the hurt, too—if I didn't care, it all wouldn't matter. But because I care, I also have something connecting me to all these people and places and things.

~

Friday morning, I wake up, and there's nothing on the news following up about my coyote. At breakfast, my family's like, *Give it a minute, the story just aired last night,* but on the bus, Owen, Leo, and I keep refreshing the WGMZ webpage, hoping for an update. As we pull into the school lot, there's still nothing.

All morning during breaks at school, I check the website, my email, texts, voicemail, everything. Still no response.

At recess, Cora comes up to me.

"The news story was pretty great," she says, her tone of voice demanding agreement.

"Yeah."

She doesn't go away. "I think it's really cool that you're doing all this to save that coyote."

"Coyotes eat dogs, you know." I feel like honesty is necessary with this girl.

She snorts. "Yeah, I realize that. I don't just repeat everything people tell me, okay? Obviously before dragging my uncle into this, I looked into the coyote thing. They're kind of a pain, but they're wild animals. They don't deserve to be punished for just being themselves. I mean, it didn't mean to hurt anyone. It was just scared."

I look up from my phone. I assumed she helped us so that she could get on TV, but hearing that, I wonder if Cora Phillips might actually care about this. "She," I say.

"What?"

"The coyote's a she," I repeat. "I found her and took care of her. I was even there when she got taken away by the animal control people."

"Oh my gosh," Cora says, and actually sits down next to me like she's interested.

So I put away my phone and tell her everything.

"Wow," she says. "That's so cool. You were trying to save her this whole time? I had no idea."

"It's kind of my fault she's in trouble."

Cora shrugs. "Could be she would've found trouble on her own. At least now, she has someone fighting on her side."

I snort a little laugh. "I hadn't thought about it that way," I say.

Cora waves her hand. "The stuff I read about coyotes, they're getting themselves into trouble all the time."

The bell rings. We both watch people begin to run for the doors.

"Thanks for helping us out, Cora," I say.

"No worries," she says. "I kind of like coyotes now. It's cool to be helping something that's not, you know, obviously what you'd pick out to help."

"It's not hard to get people on board with rescuing a cute, fluffy bunny."

"Even the cute, fluffy bunnies are not cute and fluffy all of the time," she says, getting up. "I'd like to think that in those moments, someone will have their backs, too."

She waves goodbye and trots over to her group of friends. Cora looks like a bunny, but she's got teeth — still, I'd back her up, same as she's backing me and my girl. Maybe that's the truth about all of us, about what we all need.

After school, I do one last check. Nothing on the website, no email. But then I decide to check the Fish and Wildlife Department's website.

There's a press release: *Responding to Recent Media Accounts Concerning the Rockledge Coyote.*

Eyes closed, fingers crossed, I click the link.

THIRTY-ONE
Rill

MY EYES CRACK OPEN, AND it is night.

No, not night, just darkness. I hear day birds chirping. As I lift my snout, I see pricks of light peeking through the cracks.

I am moving. No, wait, *I* am not moving, but I am in a box and it is moving me.

To where?

The terrible taste of those grits is still in my mouth. A cloud surrounds my head; my senses are all dulled. I stand and my legs hold me. There's no pain, no burning. Even the itchy feeling under my fur is better. I shake, and I feel a little better still. I stretch and my paws hit the walls of this box.

Panic creeps out and through my body. Where am I being taken? A tiny voice inside barks, *Home!*

Do I dare to even hope it?

The moving stops. There are screeching sounds and thumping sounds, and then my dark box heaves itself up and I am thrown into the walls.

The box drops and stops moving. I settle my stomach, find my footing. I am ready to pounce on whatever is coming.

The wall of the box in front of me slides up and—it's forest. Trees, dirt, leaves, wind, water on the air—yes, it's a forest!

I step tentatively forward. Glance from side to side—no humans. I trot out of the box, sniff the air. Not only is this *a* forest, this is *my* forest.

There's a noise behind me, and I see the humans disappear inside a metal mover. So there were humans. I lope away from them, checking over my shoulders every few strides.

But they don't follow. Their mover shrinks behind me, and then disappears as I drop down over a ledge.

I am free.

I am free and I am strong and I am back home in my forest —*Mother, Father, Fern, Sand, Pebble, Birch!*

My yips echo through the trees, bounce off the rocks, sending my howl all over the forest.

But there is no response.

And then I remember that my family is not here, that Teeth

had found them, and that they were in some strange human place. A place not meant for coyotes.

I have to find Teeth.

~

The first relief is that I pick up Teeth's scent, and it's only a day old. Which means he wasn't hurt by my family or any other coyote. Which means he's okay.

But this relief soon ebbs: for someone who's so smelly, Teeth is hard to track. I have to sniff around in circles until I find where he left the heights in the trees and then follow him again until the scent disappears up yet another clump of trees.

It's both so strange and so wonderful to be moving about my forest, to be able to lope in any direction and not hit a wall of twigs, to no longer be trapped in that cave by pain and injury. And yet under all the joy and excitement is the thought of my family, missing from our forest.

Where are you, Teeth?

What if he's at the cave? I had left food there. Maybe he's found it. Maybe he's using my cave to hide more food.

I should go check.

The cave was up high, in the burned place. I shy at stepping onto the blackened ground, but there's no way it's still hot. I know that—how could it be hot after so long? The humans were walking on it when I was taken. But my paws remember the pain.

I step lightly. Not hot. I place another paw onto the black ground, then another. The earth is cool and dry. I lope up the hills and ledges, along the paths, and soon smell my own scent—oh dear, I left quite a scent trail after being trapped for so long.

The cleft in the rock is smaller than I remember it, the slope at its far end shallower. But the scent does not lie—this is where my life nearly ended.

I scent the air, and there is a whiff of Teeth's odor, but that could be old. I look into the crevice, but it's cloudy and I can't see all the way inside. So I must go down there. I never wanted to be down there again.

My paws slide on pebbles, and I land with an ungraceful thud in front of what had been my hiding hole for so many suns. And there, snoozing away in the shadows, is Teeth.

"You know, any predator could just sneak up and eat you," I yip loudly.

"Gah!" Teeth startles and then passes out, emitting his terrible stink.

Do not wake an unsuspecting opossum!

"Bleh," he says, rousing himself after a few minutes. "Oh, it's you." He scratches his tail, checks his whiskers for dirt. "Nice to scare a guy half to death as a greeting."

"I forgot about your . . . problems."

"Not *problems*," he says, pointing a pink claw at me.

"Defensive techniques carefully developed over generations that have kept my species going since the moon started rising."

I snuffle a pant. "All right, all right. I forgot about your *defensive techniques*."

He waddles out from the small cave where I had hidden myself. "You look better. What happened? One night I leave you here, trapped as usual, and the next time I come by, you're gone!"

"Well, it wasn't entirely my choice to leave." I tell him the whole story about my capture, the boxes, the fake suns and false forest. "The new humans helped me, too," I yip, "and they brought me back here. Teeth," I say, lowering my chest so I can look him in his eyes, "did you find my family?"

He rubs behind his ears. "You sure you want to go back with them?" he asks. "We had a good thing going here. Could be, we make a longer-term deal?" His beady black eyes shine in the dim light.

"I thought opossums were born to wander the woods on their own?"

He shrugs, twitches his whiskers. "Maybe not all opossums."

I pant at this.

"What's so funny?" he hisses, getting defensive.

"Okay, okay," I yip. "Don't get your tail in a knot. I'm open to negotiations. But first, we find the rest of the pack."

"Oh, no. I'm not joining up with those coyotes," Teeth says. "You want to be in that pack, you're on your own."

"What pack?" I yip. "My family pack?"

He nods, wipes a paw across his snout. "I managed to get close enough to ask one. They raised their hackles and growled something fierce, but one young pup yipped, 'How do you know Rill?,' so I assumed these coyotes were at least related."

A thrill shivers up from my tail. They're alive!

"Where, Teeth?" I bark, impatient to see them, to smell them, to feel their fur against mine.

Teeth sits back on his haunches. "It's not far, but it's not a good place. I want to be straight with you: I don't think it's safe for you to go there."

"What do you mean?" I ask.

"Because it's a fully human space they're hiding in. A flat space of dirt with big, hulking metal human things rolling around on parallel bars. The humans there leave poison traps around. I've seen my fair share of sick and dying rats in that place. So no way the humans would let a pack of coyotes live there without taking some defensive action to protect their metal rollers.

"When I say it's not safe for you, I mean it's not safe, period. And especially for a coyote like you who's just recovered from a terrible sickness that had you hiding in a hole for nearly a full moon cycle."

Poison traps? Think of an idiot like Fern. He'd eat poison and not know it until he was dead on his paws. And giant metal rollers? What if one crushed Father's paw? Or trapped Sand's tail?

"Please, Teeth," I whimper. "I have to get to them. I have to help them, no matter the danger."

Teeth cleans his whiskers, wipes his paws on his belly. "All right," he squeaks. "We'll travel there tonight—it's too dangerous by day. But don't say I didn't warn you."

THIRTY-TWO
Gabe

"WE DID IT!" SCREAMS LEO. "WE. DID. IT." He starts chanting the three words, and soon there are a couple people standing around chanting along with him.

I hold up my phone and add, "The coyote is saved!"

Somehow—well, because of Cora—everyone knows what I'm talking about. There's a round of applause and whoops and cheers, and then everyone's in on the chant: *WE DID IT! WE DID IT! WE DID IT!* Cora looks over at me and smiles. I smile back.

The teachers start trying to shoo everyone to their buses and waiting parents, but they're all checking their phones, wanting to read the words for themselves.

The Department wants to thank all the people who came

together to support the Rockledge Coyote. This female coyote came into the care of the Department based on her being discovered in the park after hiding for several weeks in an underground cave. We were able to determine the date of her injuries because the animal had severe burns resulting from the Rockledge Fire.

We are pleased to inform the public that the coyote has now recovered. Additionally, it has been determined that the animal is releasable. An animal is only releasable if it will have the ability to return to its wild life and have an optimal chance of surviving.

The Department's policy on coyotes is that if they are releasable and if there is no evidence of their being either rabid or having become a nuisance animal or otherwise become too comfortable with humans, they may be released. This animal was deemed to have met the Department's criteria, and was therefore released this morning into its native habitat.

~

I find Zach at Veterans Park and practically smash my phone screen into his face. "We did it!"

He pushes me back, laughing. "Okay, dude, I saw." He holds a hand out to me. "Good work."

I take his hand. "Thanks."

"Enough chitchat," he says, slapping me on the shoulder.

"We've got gravel to shovel." He hands me a Parks Department vest.

"Aye, aye, Captain," I say.

~

As I'm leaving, I hear some kids on the playground—angry voices, shouting. *Not in my park,* I think. I am a junior forester after all. I walk over to the playground and see a couple older guys roughing up another kid. I get closer and see the kid is Taylor.

"Leave him alone," I say, stepping out of the shadows, my phone held in front of me, recording.

One of the bigger guys looks at me, sees the vest, the phone. "Let's go," he says to his cronies, and they shuffle off.

I hold my free hand out to Taylor. "You okay?"

He pushes himself up. "You didn't have to do that."

"No," I say, "I didn't. But I don't let bullies get away with stuff anymore." I turn off my phone and start back toward my bike. When I ride out of the park, Taylor's still standing there, alone. I almost feel bad for the dude. Almost.

~

I come home to find that my parents have strung streamers around the kitchen.

"Congratulations!" Mom screams, and wraps me in a hug. "Oh, the burgers!" She releases me and runs out to the patio.

Dad turns a burner off under the pot of baked beans and comes over to whack me on the back. "Nice job, buddy."

"Thanks," I manage, though he's nearly smacked the air out of my lungs.

"I made a cake," Liz says, holding a hand out to the frosted deliciousness on the counter. On top, there's *Coyote Free!* in green icing on a light blue background. "That orange box in the corner?" she says, pointing on the cake. "It's a coop."

"Oh," I say, "yeah, definitely." It looks more like a Cheez-It.

She shoves me in the shoulder. "Don't make me beat you."

I shove her back. "Just tell me, is it chocolate?"

She hugs me around the shoulder. "Is there any other kind of cake?"

Mom comes in from outside, grilled burgers on a cutting board. "Let's eat!"

Dinner is delicious. The cake—even better.

~

We hang out late watching some movie from when Mom and Dad were younger that they swear is "so great," but was a little slow, to be honest. Still, it's nice to watch a movie together, even if it's a lame movie.

When I check my phone before bed, I see Mrs. Fischer posted a comment with a ton of balloon and smiley emojis to my

Instagram of the warden's press release. There's a phone message from Mr. Larkin, which just says "Great job, Gabe." I have a bunch of congratulations and emoji-laden texts from people —Owen and Leo, Cora, some random kids I barely know, and even Ophelia Kirk—and some emails, including one from Ms. Andrews.

> Hi Gabe,
> We've scheduled your exit meeting for next week. Wednesday at 4 p.m.
> I heard about the coyote—congratulations! Nevertheless, I hope you found a way to ground yourself.
> See you Wednesday!

I write her back to let her know that works for me. I add at the end, *Don't worry—I found a rope to hold on to in case things go south.*

"Go to bed, buddy," Mom yells, knocking on my door as she passes in the hall.

"I am," I say, hitting send.

"Yeah," says Liz from the bathroom across the hall, "it's tuck-in time."

"It's tuck-in time for you, too, missy," Dad says as he comes up the stairs.

THIRTY-THREE
Rill

I HAVE NEVER TRAVELED SO far beyond the boundaries of the forest.

Teeth waddles in front of me, guiding me along a human path made of crushed stone stuck together with some kind of resin, like sap, only awful and stinking.

"Would you keep up?" he hisses at me over his shoulder.

I scuttle up behind him, but I immediately begin to fall behind. I'm shuffling along, eyes and ears and nose scanning every which way for danger. For people. I can't stand tall—what if they see me?

"Look, Rill, this is ridiculous," Teeth squeaks. "You can walk like a normal coyote. It's the middle of the night. Any human that's out now is not looking to trap you."

"If not that, then they're looking to do something worse," I whimper. I imagine the fire sticks.

We continue on in silence. Above us, every few stretches, there's a false sun shining down with dim, orangish light. Dead leaves blow across the path, some crunching under my paws. The path swerves toward the lake, and the wind rises, blowing my fur flat against my skin, sending shivers over the whole of me. Worse, with this wind, my nose is useless, and my hearing is dulled by the rush of air.

I'm going to my pack, I whisper in my mind. *I must save my family.*

"We're here," Teeth says finally.

We're still on the stone path, only now it has swung away from the lake. There's a stretch of grass and trees and rocks giving us some shelter from the wind. On the opposite side, next to the path, is a solid wall of wood planks, taller than a human, and between the two, some scrubby weeds, a tree, and a false sun on its tall, metal stem.

I sniff the air, swivel my ears. Nothing. "How can we be there? There's nothing here."

Teeth sniffs, cleans his whiskers. "Well, by here, I mean, I'm at the place where I climbed that wall"—he swings a claw at the wall of wood planks—"using this tree"—he pats the tree with his paw—"and found your family on its other side."

I feel the growl building in my throat. "Teeth," I manage. "You know I can't climb trees."

He shrugs. "You wanted me to take you to your family—this is the best I can do."

"This can't be it," I growl. "This can't be the end."

"Scruffy," Teeth snaps. "You're a coyote. Coyotes problem-solve." He walks up to the wall. "You could jam one paw on the tree and scramble up between the two." He's looking at the wall, scratching his head.

Opossums, I grumble. I sniff along the wall, jab a paw at it every few paces. The dirt is hard—no way I can dig through by sunrise. The wood is solid. I can't believe I've come so far only to be stopped by a wall. I slam my front paws against it.

And it moves.

I drop back, heart suddenly racing. "Teeth, Teeth!" I yip. "Here, the wall, it's weaker."

He waddles over. "Huh." He pokes the wood plank, bites at it. Then he runs his little body against the plank and it shifts slightly. "Can you squeeze through?" he asks.

"I'll have to," I snap. I lean back and then thrust my shoulder into the plank. I wriggle and nose and bite and dig and claw and shove and push and squeeze and wriggle more and then *SNAP!*

The bottom of the plank gives way and drops off, leaving a small coyote-sized hole in the wooden wall.

"Nice," Teeth says, waddling under the broken plank. "I'll give you this, Rill, you're tenacious."

"Tena-what?" I snarl, licking my shoulder, which throbs with dull pain.

"You have grit. You follow through. You say you're going to do something, and you do it." He nods, smiling.

I give him a half-smile. "Okay, then, I'll take it." I shake, settle my paws on this dry, dusty dirt. I sniff the air, and it stinks of human smells, but there, on the weak breeze from the direction of sunrise, I smell coyote. "Let's move," I yip, and race toward the scent.

There's a stretch of weedy, dusty ground, and then two, long —endless!—metal vines stretched over evenly spaced chunks of trees. On the vines rest the hulking metal rollers Teeth had mentioned.

"Slow down!" he says, wheezing as he shuffles up beside me. "Now's when you have to sneak, Rill. Over there." He points across the dark grounds, and between the deep shadows of other hulking rollers, I see a human structure with its false suns gleaming.

"There are people there?" I yip. I had not counted on humans being present during my rescue attempt.

Teeth shrugs, still trying to catch his breath. "Maybe? They're there during the day. And the light's on."

Burrs and prickers, I growl to myself. And I thought the

worst part was going to be trying to squeeze Father through that hole in the wall . . .

"Who's there?" The growl is deep and fierce.

"Father?" I whimper, the yip escaping my jowls before I think better of it.

A shadow steps out from between the hulking metal boxes. "Who's there?" he asks again, his yip now questioning, tentative.

"Oh, Father," I wail, "it's me, Rill!" I run toward him, not caring if the humans see me, because I found them!

Father leaps and prances around me, sniffing me and licking my fur. "We worried you were burned in the fire, but we hoped you were long gone before it started," he whimpers. "Mother convinced herself you'd left the park to find your own territory. That you were far from us and safe. But then this rodent told us you were still in the park. We didn't believe a squeak of it, but here you are! We never would have left if we thought—if there was even a chance." His yips fall off and he nuzzles my ruff. "Oh, my girl, my girl," he whuffles into my fur.

"Father," I yip back, hugging my body to his.

"Come," he says, panting. "We must tell your mother."

"What about Fern, Sand? Did Birch get lost in the ledges again?"

Father waves his tail. "No, we all made it out. We've been living in different places outside the forest." He begins loping into the darkness and I follow. He continues, "We tried to hide in different human places, but got chased off or scared away. This place is quiet most nights. We stay hidden during the day."

He leads me toward a stack of wooden boxes, all only slightly larger than the one the humans used to move me. "We've made a den under here," he says, and swings his nose into the shadows.

Then he jerks straight up, nose in the air. "Something's followed us," he growls.

I sniff around, suddenly alert, but then realize I forgot to introduce him. "Don't worry, Father," I yip. "It's only my pack-mate, Teeth."

As I say his name, the opossum waddles out from under the hulking metal box on the vines. "Hello there," he squeals.

"The rodent? You've made a pack with it?" Father is now growling at me.

I glance at Teeth, who looks ready to pass out and stink himself. "Teeth helped me find you," I explain. "I would have never known you survived without him. So stop growling." I end on a firm yip, and Father pulls his snout back, a bit shocked, perhaps, at my defense of Teeth.

"Well, then," he yips in a snarky tone. "He can wait here." He ducks his head and slips into the den.

I shake my snout. "Coyotes aren't in general friendly with opossums," I say to Teeth as a kind of apology.

Teeth waves a paw, dismissing my concern. "I've been

greeted with worse," he squeaks. "At least he didn't try to eat me."

I snuffle a pant. "I'll be right back," I yip. I follow my Father's scent into the den.

Inside, I find Mother and my brothers and sister all curled up. My heart pounds, seeing them safe.

My pack is back together.

"Rill?" Mother yips, her eyes opening. She smells weak. I'm guessing these have been hard times for my family.

"I'm here, Mother," I yip, and curl myself beside her, rubbing into her body. I can feel her ribs against my spine. "I'm here to lead you back to the forest," I yip. "It's safe now, and the prey has returned."

"Prey?" yips one of my brothers. And then all the pups are yipping about food. I squeeze myself back outside, and they all follow me.

"Rill!" yips Sand. "It's Rill!" And then they're all yipping and howling and making a fuss, jumping around me. I should tell them to be quiet, but I find I'm yipping and howling along with them.

"The humans!" shrieks Teeth, and he scuttles under the metal roller.

I stop barking and swivel my ears—yes, I hear them. Over by the false suns. "Father, Mother," I yip quietly. "We must go, now."

They look at each other, then Mother nods. "We'll follow you," she yips.

I lope lightly, moving from shadow to shadow, hoping the darkness will protect us from the humans. My family follows tightly behind me.

KA-PLOW!

The dirt just in front of my snout bursts into dust and pebbles.

"Fire sticks!" Father screams and bolts ahead.

Fear freezes my paws—what happened to Boulder and Maple is happening again—but then I shake it off. Fear will not blind me this time.

"Hurry!" I yip to my family. I race toward the wall, diving through the darkness, hoping that if I move fast enough, the fire stick can't catch me.

KA-PLOW!

I hear the explosion of earth behind me, hear my siblings yelp in fear. But they are racing beside me. We are so close! Father hits the wall and begins trying to squeeze through.

Then there's a yelp behind me: "My paw!"

It's Fern.

I turn and see him struggling against the ground, his paw held in some snag of roots. I race over, jaws ready to jerk his paw out, but then I see that it is not a root. This is a metal mouth, a curling, snapping human trap.

"Help me!" Fern whimpers.

My family shoves at Father, trying to push him through the broken wood. "Come on, Rill!" Sand cries.

I will not leave this time. "Stop struggling," I snap at Fern.

Fern freezes, paw trembling in panic. I sniff the trap, lick it, bite it, feel the tension in its jaws. If only I could open them . . .

Teeth slides to a halt beside me. "Rill, we have to go."

KA-PLOW! The fire stick blasts a hole in the fence near where my family is struggling.

"Not without my brother," I snap. I turn pleading eyes to Teeth. "Please help me. Use your paws," I say. "Push the metal jaws apart with me."

Teeth hesitates, but then he nods. He takes one side, and I the other. I bite and tug, forcing my fangs between the jaws of the trap, and Teeth jams his body in, pushing one side with his arms and one with his feet.

It starts to move. We need more strength, though. "Mother! Father! Help me!" I yip.

They're still digging at the fence, trying to squeeze through.

"I can't push any harder!" Teeth squeals.

"Birch, Sand, please!" I howl. "We have to do this together!"

And then my Mother is there beside me. "Together!" she yips. She shoves her paw in and pulls with Teeth. Pebble, Sand, and Birch appear, and they tug, too. Finally Father joins us, and with his giant paw pushing down on the trap, Fern is able to jerk back and slips free. We all release the trap and jump away, avoiding its snap.

"We did it!" I cry.

"You did it," Father says, looking in wonder from Fern's paw, to the trap, to me.

"We did it," says Teeth, smiling up at us all. "Together."

KA-PLOW! The fire stick blows another hole in the wall, expanding my broken plank into a true escape hatch.

"Run!" I howl, and my family follows me through the enlarged hole and out onto the rock path. We race down the path, not stopping until we reach the full darkness near the lake, until the wind hides our scent and sound.

There are no more explosions from the fire stick. No scent of human on the wind. *We're safe.*

Teeth nearly charges into us. "You made it!" he cries. "I can't believe it, but you made it!"

I can't believe it, either, but we did. We made it. We're safe.

"Let's go home," I yip.

Father licks Fern, then bows his head to me. "Lead the way."

~

As the sun rises, we find one of our old dens, one outside the fire's reach. Mother sneaks inside, checks the space. "It's safe," she says, ears high, tail waving, "but some rodents have been here, so there's cleaning out to do." She ducks back into the den.

"A squirrel!" Birch barks, and he races into the trees.

"Save a bite for me!" yips Fern. Father chases after them, hoping to save the meal. Maybe we've all changed over the last moon cycle.

"I guess I'll be off," Teeth squeaks, dropping down to all fours.

"Thank you," I yip, and sneak a lick on the top of his head.

He hisses, straightens the fur around his ears. "Hey, now, don't go all slobbery on me."

"Not slobbery, just grateful for a packmate."

He smiles, his pointy teeth sparkling. "A packmate, eh?" He plays with the end of his tail. "Maybe, as packmates, we could sniff out some trash sometime. When the humans are back." He glances over. I sense this is a gift, the offer of sharing some human scraps.

"I'd love that," I yip, and lick him again, just to get him squealing.

"No slobbering!" He shuffles off into the brush, shaking like I doused him in drool.

Mother steps out of the den, lopes to me, and begins grooming my fur. "I'm sorry we left you behind, Rill."

"I left *you*," I yip. "I thought I wanted to set out on my own."

"You've changed your mind?" Mother says, jowls lifting.

Somewhere in the woods, there's a cacophony of yips—the runts most likely bungling the squirrel hunt. "I'm sure you could use my help."

Father lopes out from between some bushes. "We sure could," he yips. "Those pups nearly lost the first piece of prey we've had cornered." He drops some meat at my paws.

"For me?" I cannot believe I'm being offered meat, especially when I didn't hunt, especially from Father.

"You've done more for this pack than any scraps of meat could ever repay."

I hear my siblings fighting in the woods over the squirrel, and Mother and Father trot into the trees to separate them.

"Rill!" howls Pebble. "Fern says it's his squirrel, but I'm the one who caught the tail!"

"Fern," I bark, "you know the rules: everyone who lends a paw can claim the catch." I take up the meat, swallow it down, then race toward the bickering runts. This more than anything tells me I'm home. And there's no place else I'd rather be.

THIRTY-FOUR
Gabe

MR. DARLING CLEARS HIS THROAT, and everyone in the room stops chitchatting. Ms. Andrews said there was nothing to be nervous about, but sitting in a circle with all these people again—I'm nervous.

Mr. Darling begins, "Last time we all gathered here, we discussed the harm that Mr. Meyer's actions caused the community. Today, we're here to learn what Mr. Meyer has done to repair that harm."

Zach talks about my community service hours. Mr. Davis confirms that I paid my restitution in full. Mr. Larkin tells how I helped him rebuild his chicken coop, even though it wasn't in the contract. Mrs. Fischer gabs about our quest to save the coyote until Ms. Andrews cuts her off.

"Now, we'll hear from Mr. Meyer."

I stand, pick up my papers, look around at all the faces—Mr. Larkin; Mrs. Fischer and her family, including her daughter; Zach, Owen, and Leo; my family—take a deep breath, and begin.

"I want to thank you all for coming here today. I am proud of what I have done to complete my contract with you. I paid the restitution I owed to Mr. Davis. Mr. Davis, I'm sorry that I took the fireworks from your store."

My hands are shaking. Man, I'm glad I wrote this yesterday.

"To all the members of the community who were affected by the fire. I'm sorry that I lit those fireworks. I didn't think they would do anything more than shoot a few sparkles. The problem really is that I didn't *think*. I just lit the fireworks. I didn't consider the consequences.

"Through this process, I've learned to consider consequences. I've learned to take a moment and think, What's the worst that could happen?"

I get to the next part and tears fill my eyes. I can't read, so I just try to wing it. "I hurt people's homes; I hurt the park itself. I've tried to fix what I could. Not only through my community service with Zach, but I'm also doing extra hours to fix the park. I started building chicken coops to raise money to replace the picnic pavilion. I remember having picnics there with my mom. I want other kids to be able to have picnics there, too.

"But the worst part is that I hurt the animals in the park.

There was this coyote—she was so injured, she almost didn't make it. The fire scared her so badly, she raced into Mrs. Fischer's yard and snapped at her kid. That was a consequence of my actions. Something I never could have guessed would happen.

"And then she was going to be put down for that. Another consequence."

I take a deep breath, put the papers down. "I guess I've learned that it's not just thinking about what I'm doing and what *I* want, but how what I'm doing affects other people and animals and plants—everything. That I'm a part of something bigger, and that means I can't do just anything. And it also means I'm not alone.

"That's the biggest thing I've gained from this experience. I know that I have friends in the community. I owe it to them to be the best member of the community that I can." I had that last part memorized, just in case.

Mr. Darling nods, smiling. "Thank you, Mr. Meyer."

The meeting ends, and a bunch of people come up to shake hands with me. Some don't, and that's okay—I can't force people to forgive me. But the people who do stay talk about seeing me on the news. They say they're proud of me. What's cool is, I'm proud of myself. Not just for not passing out while speaking in front of all these people, but I actually feel really good about what I've accomplished. I am sorry for what I did, but I also feel really good about everything I've done since then.

Owen and Leo come up and high-five me. "Nice job," Owen says.

"My mom edited it to sound 'more professional,'" I admit.

"It was good," Owen says. "Really *awesome*."

They both look at me.

"Don't leave us hanging," Leo says, cocking his head.

I snort a laugh, then put my fingers up and do a little fake dance as I say, *"Allen."*

"You guys are freaks," Liz says, coming over to us. She hugs me. "You did great."

Mom is talking to Ms. Andrews. Mr. Larkin and Dad are answering questions about the chicken coops—business is booming. It's weird remembering how awful and cold this room felt the first time I came in here. Now, it's just a room full of people who cared enough to make me care.

~

Thursday, Zach has me back at Rockledge resetting some rails on the edge of a trail near the lake on the west side of the park. It's gotten cold, so I'm wearing gloves under my work gloves and a hat and my neck warmer. There aren't many people out today. The wind off the lake is making the cold, like, a thousand times worse.

I slam the shovel in and manage to shift the heavy branch back into the groove I dug for it. *Done.*

Heading back toward the ranger station to return the

shovel, I clear a ridge and hear something behind me. Across the gully, a pack of coyotes is silhouetted in the dim light. I freeze, my heart pounds. I've never seen a coyote in the wild, not since my coyote . . .

One stops, looks back at me. I stare into the shadows, wanting to know: Is it my girl?

The coyote swings its head, looks out over the lake, then follows the pack down into the shadows. I watch her until she's gone.

I turn around, begin tromping down the path to head out. I hear a yip. Two yips.

I stop, look around. Nothing.

More yips, and then it's like a rock band of coyotes, filling the entire park with yips and howls.

I bet they caught something. I bet they're celebrating an awesome coyote-caught dinner.

"Good job, girl!" I shout back to them.

No way they heard me—they're still yipping—but I have a smile on my face all the way out of the park.

AUTHOR'S NOTE

Wayward Creatures began with the idea of writing the story of an animal and a boy who on the surface were not very likable. I knew who my boy was right away—he was angry at the world, and the people in his world did not know what to do with him and his anger. I then began looking for the perfect animal to connect with his story. When I came across the coyote, I knew the search was over.

America has an uncomfortable history with the coyote, also called the "song dog," which, as a singer myself, I love. Coyotes are unique to North America, having developed from an early wolflike ancestor some 800,000 years ago. They are cunning predators with complex family groups and social dynamics. However, after the Civil War, the coyote's predatory presence on the western plains made them enemies of the developing ranching industry. As a result, coyotes were hunted as a part of official extermination programs up through the late twentieth century.

People really didn't like coyotes! According to a 1980 Yale University study, people in the United States ranked coyotes as the least appealing wild creature, behind even rats and cockroaches. Only very recently has public opinion changed regarding coyotes, and they are now understood to be a part of a balanced ecosystem. This, to me, mirrored in some general ways how the public's understanding of angry kids who act out has started to change, and how the criminal justice system has evolved to address these changing views, including embracing restorative justice practices.

I work in the criminal court, so I assumed I had a good sense of what restorative justice was about. Thank goodness I talked to the director of the Burlington Community Justice Center, Rachel Jolly! She not only talked to me about her program but explained how very different it was from what I was used to in the criminal courts, not just procedurally but philosophically.

1: What is restorative justice?

Restorative justice is an alternative to how communities handle crimes in modern western legal systems. In a typical

American county, when someone is accused of a crime but the person says they are innocent, a trial is held in a court before a jury of regular citizens from the community. The government has to prove to the jury that that person committed the crime. The person also gets a chance to prove that they didn't commit the crime. If the jury believes that the government proved that the person committed the crime, the jury finds the person guilty and then the judge decides the appropriate punishment, called a sentence.

Restorative justice isn't about punishment or proof. Restorative justice takes a totally different view of crime, seeing it as a violation of people and obligations — a breakdown of the community — and that justice means bringing those people together to repair the harm. Restorative justice is not a new methodology; rather, modern restorative practices have their roots in ancient cultures from around the world, including Native American traditions.

For example, to participate in one of Vermont's restorative justice programs, the person who committed the crime admits what they did and takes responsibility for their actions. They then work with a panel of volunteers from the community and the victim of the crime to think about how they can repair the harm caused by their crime. Together, they come up with a plan for the person who committed the crime to make things right with the victim and the community.

2: Can any crime go through restorative justice instead of the courts? Why isn't restorative justice used for all crimes?

Restorative justice is not used for all crimes in Vermont, though other states and countries have different programs that allow for even super serious crimes to be resolved through restorative practices. In Vermont, restorative justice is used when the person who committed the crime wants to make things right, and when the crime that was committed can be made right.

In real life, arson, which is the crime that was committed in this book, would not normally be recommended for restorative justice in Vermont. (In real life, Gabe probably would not have been able to commit this particular crime, as it's against the law to sell fireworks in mini-marts in Vermont.) Arson is a serious crime that often causes a lot of damage and threatens people's lives, homes, and businesses. Here, Gabe's age was one factor considered by my fictional East Burlington police and the lawyers for the government in deciding to recommend his case to the restorative justice program. But restorative justice programs are not limited to addressing juvenile crimes, or crimes committed by kids; restorative justice practices can be used to address crimes committed by adults, too.

3: How does restorative justice work?

Howard Zehr, one of the founding developers in the field, said, "Restorative justice is a compass not a map." While there are certain principles and philosophies that are common to all restorative justice programs, panels or conference circles, like those discussed in this book, are only one way to carry out these philosophies and principles. More simply, restorative justice provides a way of thinking about what to do after a crime happens, but the choice of what to do is left to the individual community.

In Vermont, the first thing that happens is that the crime, which is called a case, is transferred out of the traditional criminal justice system. This can happen early in the case by the police officer or later by the government lawyer or the judge. The person who committed the crime, and their family if they're a kid, is given a referral to the community justice center, and then someone from the community justice center contacts them to set up an intake meeting. Usually, this takes several weeks, but for the purposes of this story, I shortened the timeline to a few days.

The purpose of the intake meeting is to introduce the kid and their family to the restorative justice process and to get to know the person. Once they feel comfortable, the conversation shifts to talking about the incident: What happened? What did the person do? How were they feeling? Who was affected? What needs to be done to make things right? The person is told that the people impacted by the crime will be contacted, but that everything they just talked about won't be shared with anyone, including the impacted parties.

The next step is the initial panel. The person who committed the crime comes together with the impacted party and a panel of trained volunteers from the community. Everyone sits in a circle because everyone should be seen, and seen as an equal. Everyone comes to the panel with the mindset that they are responsible for their actions and the intention to figure out how they can play a role in making sure this doesn't happen again.

The panel proceeds in a similar way to the intake meeting. Everyone introduces themselves, and then typically the person responsible for the crime, the responsible party, talks about what happened and what they did. The victim, or impacted party, shares how what happened made them feel; sometimes the victim doesn't want to participate, and a victim impact statement—a letter from the victim telling the responsible party their experience of the crime—is read instead. And then everyone collaborates on coming up with a plan called a "restorative justice agreement" for how the responsible party can make things right. The plan can be anything from community service, to paying back money that was stolen or paying to fix what was broken, to a written apology letter published anonymously in the local newspaper. (Everything in restorative justice is confidential.)

Next, the responsible party does what they promised to do

in the agreement. There can be a check-in meeting with the panel to see how the person is progressing. The last step is the final meeting with the whole panel and the impacted party. At the final meeting, the responsible party confirms that they completed what they promised to do in the agreement, providing some kind of proof that they did it, like a photograph or signed statement from their community service supervisor.

Again, this is only one type of restorative justice program. Restorative justice programs are as different as the communities they serve. The program described above and as represented in this book is based on the program in Burlington, Vermont.

4: But, wait a second, what about punishing the person for what they did?

Restorative justice is not about punishment or making someone feel bad for what they did. Restorative justice is a relationship-based approach to conflict: there's a person who did something that has hurt someone else in the community, and that person wants to make things right, the hurt person wants things to be made right, and things can be made right. They come together with members of the community to figure out how the responsible party can repair the hurt.

Even in the regular criminal justice system, punishment is only one goal of sentencing. For example, when a judge sentences a convicted criminal, they consider, among other factors, how the person who committed the crime can be rehabilitated so that they can come back into the community after they have served their sentence.

5: How can I learn more about restorative justice in my community?

You can check with your local police department or court to see if there's a restorative justice program in your community and how it works. If there's no program in your community, you can look into what's been done in other communities by searching online. You can also read books about restorative justice. A good place to start might be *The Little Book of Restorative Justice* by Howard Zehr.

There are even youth panels led by kids in some places, where kids are trained to run restorative justice panels for crimes committed by other kids. Check out the Center for Court Innovation's Youth Court page at www.courtinnovation.org/programs/youth-court. There's a great video on that page about the Newark Youth Court. Also, sometimes schools run restorative justice programs to resolve conflicts. Check out *It Wasn't Me* by Dana Alison Levy for a fictional example of how this might work.

If you'd like to learn more about coyotes, especially urban coyotes, you can check out *A Pup Called Trouble* by Bobbie

Pyron, which is a novel based on the true story of the coyotes living in Central Park in New York City. If you're looking for a seriously in-depth look at the North American coyote and its history, check out *Coyote America* by Dan Flores, which is where I learned the facts noted in this section.

ACKNOWLEDGMENTS

The seed of this book was developed in collaboration with my amazing editor, Amy Cloud. Thank you so much for your insight and encouragement, for your keen eye for what could be cut—you made the whole book come into focus with your edits!—and for suggesting fireworks.

Thank you to the whole team at Clarion Books for helping to make this book a reality, especially Helen Seachrist, Kaitlin Yang, Emma Grant, and Taylor McBroom. Special thanks to my fabulous publicist, Sammy Brown. And thank you to Junyi Wu for creating such a beautiful cover—you captured the connection between Gabe and Rill, and the forest as a whole, so well.

Thank you, Faye Bender, for being there for me through every step of this process, and for guiding me so expertly. I am lucky to have an agent such as you by my side.

On the subject of experts, I relied on the in-depth knowledge of others to fill in holes in my research. Thanks to my county forester, Ethan Tapper, for helping me to understand forests as a system. Thank you especially to Rachel Jolly, director of the Burlington Community Justice Center, for all your help getting my brain off the criminal court track and onto the restorative justice line. Your input and advice were essential to helping me get this story right. Thanks also to Kelly Ahrens, manager of the Youth Restorative Justice Program at the Burlington CJC. I apologize for any inaccuracies — they are my own, either through my misunderstanding or the needs of the story.

Thank you to my fantastic critique partners, Rachel Carter and Margot Harrison. You guys are the best readers a writer could ask for, and always have spot-on advice for how to make my writing better. Thank you, Mom, for your support and encouragement, and for reading drafts of every one of my books. And thank you to the Kindling Words community for your early support of the first pages of this story.

Finally, thank you to my family for inspiring me and supporting me, for laughing with me and offering a hug when I needed one. Thanks especially to my husband, Jason, on this one — I couldn't have gotten the story right without your input.